-84   0

2-8A

Murder Among Friends

Murder
Among Friends

Frank McConnell

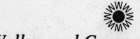

Walker and Company, New York

*For Carolyn as always
and for Stuart Kaminsky, friend and critic*

   *First published in the United States of America
in 1983 by the Walker Publishing Company, Inc.*

   *Published simultaneously in Canada by John Wiley & Sons
Canada, Limited, Rexdale, Ontario.*

Library of Congress Catalog Card Number: 83-42741.

Printed in the United States of America

10 9 8 7 6 5 4 3 2 1

Library of Congress Cataloging in Publication Data

*McConnell, Frank D., 1942-
  Murder among friends.*

  *I. Title.
PS3563.C3437M8 1983   813'.54   83-42741
ISBN 0-8027-5567-4*

•1

FRED shivered. He was cold, nervous, and very sleepy. He had been standing beside his car for an hour and it was one in the morning, in the middle of February, in the middle of the north Chicago suburbs. The Skokie parking lot of the Chicago Transit Authority, where he was waiting, was, for most of the working day, a shoal of beached cars. They lay there to be reclaimed by their commuter-owners, on their way home to neat little houses full of neat little children, neat little wives, and early martinis. The rich, he thought, didn't have to stand in the cold, in the dark, for meetings that would shame them. So they paid other people for that kind of meeting. Screw the rich, he thought—and took another sip from the pint of vodka in his overcoat pocket.

It tasted worse this time than the last, made him grimace like he had a tin knife between his teeth. And it didn't warm him. It had chilled in his pocket, a supercooled icecube. He felt the cold burn his esophagus on the way down.

He was drifting. He was dreaming about times he had been warm and happy. Long ago. He blinked himself awake again, and checked his watch. One-thirty, and his contact had been for twelve-thirty. The lot was empty except for a few scattered cars whose owners had found better things to do in the city; or maybe had died today. Out of five hundred random car owners, he wondered, how many were likely to have a heart attack, step in front of a speeding car, or blow their brains out on any given day? You could probably look it up somewhere. Insurance salesmen could tell you without thinking.

A three-week-old snow was still on the ground, trampled, pureed, and refrozen into dirty marble. You could walk on it or drive on it with no problem, until you hit that special patch reserved for you, the one patch that's slicker than the others. And then you would fall on your butt or skid into an oncoming, brand-new Olds. And the other guy would be uninsured. That's what Chicago winters were about. He had seen forty-two of them.

Drifting again, he thought, and swore aloud—more to keep himself awake than for any other reason. And here I am, he thought, a quarter of a century at the job, thinking phony-deep thoughts like a kid who's read Raymond Chandler for the first time. Well, but wasn't it stories like that which had once, so long ago, made the business seem so attractive, so full of the possibility of romance? But Chicago wasn't Chandler's Los Angeles—neither was Los Angeles—and anyway, Chandler was a liar.

The job was not only dirty and risky, it was pointless and addictive. Playing around for pay in the lives of other people—even people who deserved trouble—made you feel mean. But you got stuck doing what you did. After a while you were more afraid to think about doing something else than you were to keep on doing what you did, even at the risk of your soul. "Midlife crisis" the magazines called it. Midlife cage was more like it.

Another half hour, he promised himself (taking another drag on the vodka bottle), and I go home. Marianne would be long asleep. He had told her not to wait up, and since they had quarrelled tonight, he was sure she wouldn't. And his son would be asleep but dangerously close to waking; better tiptoe up the stairs and drop into bed in his underclothes, rather than turn on the lights and risk a two o'clock squall, a three o'clock fight, and a whole day of drowsy bad humor. And anyway, he thought ruefully, if this job has one advantage, it's that it trains you to sneak around.

Traffic was dead at this hour. Dempster Street, just off the lot, was a main artery of the suburbs, a long web of neon advertising signs, gas stations, groceries, bars, and stores with no immediately identifiable function. But now, at this hour, with only the traffic lights signalling to no one and the forlorn lamps lighting the way for no one, the strip looked gutted—the aftermath of a battle, perhaps.

He remembered reading, as a boy, *The War of the Worlds*, and he remembered, after all those years, the image of dead London, a city emptied by the invading Martian war machines. Tonight, looking at dead Dempster Street, he knew again why the image stayed with him. It was what any city looked like if you saw it from the underside. Things grew pathetic and monstrous, truly frightening, if they were disused—playgrounds without children, bars in the morning, cities at two A.M. He had seen a lot, maybe too much, of his city at two A.M.

Not ten cars had passed since he had taken up his long wait. He had tried to count them, waiting for one to turn into the lot and pull beside his Valiant, under the area pole marked 20. He checked the time again. Damn! He would have to be in his office at nine for an appointment, and he was already beginning to feel the headache that he knew would be a throbber by then. And, worse, the appointment was about one of those cases that always made him feel like taking a shower even if it was the kind of work that kept food on his table.

A Catholic, he had never understood the haste, the glee, with which his clients seemed willing to dissolve or savage what he still thought of as a sacramental bond. He had married late, having been a careful, tense virgin in a business where virginity was the stuff of bad jokes. And, he reflected, the resulting tiny but uncrossable gap of contempt he maintained from the people whose sloppy lives he entered helped him to do his job better. "What does a priest know about fucking?" ran the punch line of an old, old joke. Well, if he was a good enough listener, he knows a lot, in fact. He had many cop friends, and noticed over the years how the most puritanical, the most uptight, of them inevitably wound up on the vice squad. One explanation, of course, was that puritans all had a secret yearning for filth. But maybe, he thought, it was just that puritans—like the vice cops, like himself— understood best how dangerous, how fatal that first slip into impulse could be. Christ would forgive you anything, his church taught. But could you forgive yourself? Infidelity could be a lot of things, but it wasn't *funny*.

His headache was getting worse, and the time was getting ridiculous. As well be hung for a sheep, he thought, and downed the bottom third of his pint in a gulp. Grinning in distaste, he threw the drained bottle across the lot. It was his secret gesture of disgust—he was normally a very cautious man—for people who kept him up, pointlessly, in the lonely and freezing night.

Wow, he thought, I *am* drunk. Informers were a rabbitish crew anyhow; he'd known some who hadn't shown up till their third or fourth assignation. This one would probably call tomorrow or the next day, full of remorse and anxious to set up another meeting— early and indoors, he devoutly hoped. "It's *hard* to be a fink," he said aloud, and laughed.

When you start laughing at your own jokes, it's time to go. He fumbled for his keys and turned to his car, hoping it would start. The battery had already been recharged twice that winter.

At that moment a Volkswagen turned into the lot, skidded briefly on the ice, and headed toward area pole 20. He paused, his hand on the door. This must be it.

The VW pulled beside him and stopped, its motor running. He could make out a dark, bundled figure behind the wheel. The door on the passenger side swung open, and he could feel the warmth billowing from the car's heater.

"You're late," he said, bending to get into the car. "How long did you think I'd wait, anyhow?"

But by the time he finished the sentence he was all the way in, had closed the door, and saw what the driver held. And could almost have laughed. All these years on the job, he thought— drudgery and dreck and never anything like a real adventure. And now here it was, adventure in an empty CTA lot, the tang of danger and the elusive scent of triumph and heroism—and he was, he knew, too tired and too drunk to meet it. Poor Marianne, he thought.

And then Fred Healey started to die.

• 2

FRED didn't make the *Chicago Tribune* that morning. Newspapers have their own timetable for important events, and it depends on press-access time more than on how important the event itself is. Blow up Philadelphia at four in the morning and you'll never make the green-stripe edition. (By the red-stripe edition, of course, they'll probably have caught you, got a confession, your high school prom photo, and an exclusive interview with your eighth grade piano teacher.)

He did, though, get a ten-second shot on the TV news—you know, the five minutes of local weather, politics, rapes, and sports they sandwich between slices of the *Today* show. Killings always go up in Chicago during the winter, mind you, and in February the supply is so rich that it's hard to get any air time at all, if publicity is your reason for icing somebody. But it's mostly domestic stuff: daddy can't take the snow in his driveway anymore, so he turns the snowshovel on mommy, the kids, and the gerbil. We even had a snowplow driver, during the blizzard of 1979, who freaked out one night and coasted up and down State Street ramming the bejeezus out of illegally parked cars. The bastard could probably have run for mayor—it's what we all wanted to do, that winter—but some jerk was sleeping it off in the very last—the *very last*—car he totaled. There's always a hitch, am I right?

Nevertheless, old Fred made the news. Really crazy killings are always good copy, and Fred's was definitely not garden variety, domestic stuff.

Not that I heard about it that way. Mornings, I try to read only the comic page and the basketball scores (Dondi was saving his neighbors' marriage, and DePaul was looking like UCLA in the Wooden Age). And as for TV, I like to watch the cartoons on

5 •

Channel Nine with my poached eggs. I was in luck that day, too: they showed *One Froggy Evening*, a Warner Brothers classic and my all-time favorite. I get enough bad news when I go to work.

And the bad news was there all right when I checked in, eight-thirty on the dot, at O'Toole Investigative Agency, Inc., in the heart of Evanston, Illinois. It came with my coffee and doughnuts. It came with my boss, Bridget O'Toole, who in the two years she had been my boss had brought me more coffee and doughnuts, and more bad news, than I had ever wanted.

Not that Bridget intends, ever, to ruin your day. In fact, she "means well"—a phrase my mother used to pronounce, thin-lipped, about uncles who drank and aunts who ran off with other people's uncles. But somehow, Bridget O'Toole's well-meaning never comes out right—at least, not for me.

The complete staff of O'Toole Investigations is me, her, our receptionist Brenda who tipples on the job, and an empty office for an additional investigator we can't afford to hire full-time. For ordinary snooping and surveillance we make do with part-time help; juicers and burned-out cops, mainly, who like to skulk and can use the bread. Hard times for detective agencies; infidelity ain't what it used to be.

Anyhow, every Friday Bridget stops on her way to work and buys a dozen doughnuts for us to have with our coffee. I guess it's a hangover from her days as a schoolteacher. Remember how, after mass on the First Fridays, Sister Mary Godzilla would always trot out chocolate milk and pastries for your homeroom?

But it's a *nice* custom, I hear you saying. Except that Brenda already weighs two-fifty if she weighs an ounce, and sure as hell doesn't need any extra cholesterol, and besides that I don't *like* doughnuts. Never have.

This particular Friday morning Bridget's eyes were moist as she offered me a jelly doughnut (I especially don't like *jelly* doughnuts). "Harry, Harry," she said. "It's so awful about poor Fred. Do you think we ought to call his wife or something?"

I felt the day begin to slip out of my grasp. "Uh—Fred? Sorry, Bridget, but Fred who?" I asked, swallowing a bit of half-cooked dough. I was still—barely—in luck. I hadn't hit the jelly yet.

"Oh, no," she sighed, and sat beside me, taking the hand that didn't hold the unwanted pastry. "You haven't heard? Fred

Healey, Harry. They found him this morning, or at least they think it's Fred."

Now you see what I mean. "At least they *think* it's Fred." To a man with my finehoned deductive powers, what that means is, "Look, a good friend of yours is dead, and not only dead but murdered, and not only murdered but bashed, sawed, or mauled beyond recognition." It would say the same, of course, to a five-year-old, particularly backward, cretin.

"What do you mean, they think, Bridget?" I asked. I've always been a great one for playing out hands already lost. Besides, wide-eyed Brenda, chomping a chocolate doughnut, would have asked if I hadn't.

Bridget, by the way, is way past fifty, with a face like a cantaloupe. Right now, a concerned cantaloupe.

"Oh, dear," she said. It's her nun voice. Whenever she calls you "dear," you learn to wince. Somehow, a ruler is about to come down across your palm. "Well, it seems they found him in the back of his car, in the Skokie CTA lot. He'd been—ah—cut. He was cut apart, I mean, like with a buzz saw or something."

I put my doughnut down. It was beginning to leak jelly. Fred and I had gone to high school together, made out in the back of each other's cars on double dates, got drunk together, even gone into the same business after the Army. He had wanted to, and had talked me into it. We had both worked for old Martin O'Toole, peeping in motels and running down check jumpers, till Fred got a better offer from Northshore Detective Agency (classier motels, I guess, and bigger checks). He'd even gotten married—late. His wife was a compact brunette who was better educated and richer than he was, a college girl whose father ran a chain of liquor stores or something. He'd met her while he was snooping around for her mother's divorce. They had a kid, age five. I was god-father.

I had stayed on at O'Toole Agency, figuring I'd take over the business when old Martin retired. And then the poor old fart had had a stroke and his plain, middle-aged daughter had come out of the convent—the Sisters of the Holy Retribution, or something like that—to help "put things in order." She'd been helping put things in order for two years now. I was beginning to think she liked it.

Goodbye, *Harry Garnish Investigations, Inc.* But what could I do? Old Martin, trying to chew his soup in an expensive North Shore rest home, appeared to approve of the arrangement, and I had liked the guy too much to ruin his sunset for him. Besides, she had to leave sometime. Didn't she?

As the man said, you can't win, you can't break even, and you can't get out of the game. Or you can get out, but only one way. I didn't like to think about Fred Healey dead.

I lit a cigarette and drained my coffee. "Do the fuzz say if they have any leads?" I asked. Bridget doesn't like cigarettes and she hates to hear the fuzz called the fuzz. She withdrew her hand. Score one for H. Garnish, hard-boiled private eye.

"I don't think so, Harry. They wouldn't even have found him so soon, but poor Fred's car had its lights on. Some commuter looked in to turn them off, saw the—the body, and called the police."

Some commuter, I thought, probably lost his breakfast if the late Fred looked anything like what I imagined.

Bridget O'Toole was looking at me as if she expected something. Fat Brenda was on her third chocolate doughnut, staring at nothing in particular.

"Christ, what a shame," I said. "Do you know about the funeral? I think we ought to send flowers, at least. And I'll go, of course."

But you can't bullshit old Bridget O'Toole, especially not when you're trying to. The cantaloupe face went all odd, and she turned her gaze from me to the table. "There's been no announcement yet, but I expect the body will be at Calloran's— closed casket, of course. But, Harry"—and now she looked me in the eye again—"don't you think we should *do* something?"

I knew what was coming, and I wanted no part of it.

"Oh, hell, Bridget," I said, and rose to get myself another cup of coffee. It's bad for me, but so is working for her. "If the cops can't handle this, nobody can. You don't still think private detectives solve *crimes,* do you? Christ, you know what we do around here. So how could we help? How do we even know that Fred wasn't asking for what he got? Maybe he led a secret life. Maybe he got mixed up with some S/M people and went too far for once. It's happened, you know."

It was a nasty damned thing to say, but I wanted to make my point. Brenda blushed and rose, mumbling something about having to man the phone. On her way out she snagged cruller number four.

Bridget just stared. They really do train nuns to stare.

"Look," I said, coming back to the table with my coffee and a cup for her (how had that got there?). "This isn't any of our business, and it's plain silly to think about doing anything about it. He was an old friend, sure. And that means the best thing we can do for him is stay out of the way while the real detectives, the cops, handle this thing. Now doesn't that make sense?"

It didn't, of course. The cops in this city are about as good, I guess, as those in most others. But, as in most others, they have to *want* to be good. Otherwise they're overworked, underpaid, and bored—just like you and me. And I wasn't sure that a dead p.i., however melodramatically sliced up, would really turn out to be the stuff of which front-page collars and convictions were made. It all depended on the breaks of the news. If no planes crashed into the Sears Building for a week, and if we didn't invade Canada, it might be worth somebody's while to make a *tsimmes* out of Fred's death.

But I didn't think Bridget knew all this. One of my big problems, of course, is trying to figure out exactly what she does know, and how the hell she found it out, back there in the nunnery.

Anyway, she seemed to buy it. She sighed and got out of her chair. "Well, Harold, you're probably right. It's just that Fred did work for Father, you know, and I'm sure Father would be concerned."

"Bridget. No." I didn't smile. She did, and strode out of the room. Really, she strode—the only woman I know who can stride. It must've impressed the hell out of her fifth grade classes.

Fred had worked for "Father," she'd said. And her eyes had been moist when she'd said it. I was nervous working around people who cared, and who cared that much. Dentists don't empathize with teeth, and people in my job shouldn't do it with people. Ah, well, I told myself for the thousandth time, she had to leave sometime.

I went to my own office and began looking through the day's

schedule. It wasn't really as packed as, say, the chairman of the board's at Standard Oil. I had charge of three tailing operations— one randy wife and two randy husbands—and the retreads doing my tailing for me were all supposed to check in that afternoon. Till then, nothing to do but reread the *Tribune's* comics, maybe do the crossword puzzle, think about Fred, and think about how bad business was. Maybe, with luck, it would get bad enough that Bridget would let me buy her out. I had just enough salted away to purchase a sinking ship, provided the ship was severely enough damaged.

Then the phone rang. Or rather, two buttons lit and buzzed on my phone at the same time. One was the interoffice line, and I took that one first.

"Harry?" It was my boss. "I don't want to disturb you, dear, but I just realized something important about Fred's car."

"Uh, right, Bridget. I've got another call, but I'll come by in a minute." And I punched the next button. It was the one I'd been waiting for—not happily.

"Harry? It's Marianne Healey. Harry, I have to talk to you. Can I come in today?"

Great. Just great. And till *One Froggy Evening* ended, I'd been having a good day.

• 3

I ARRANGED to meet Fred's widow around noon, and made my reluctant way to Bridget's office.

Now I know you're not going to believe this, but Bridget's office could have been a set for *The African Queen*. Ferns hanging from the ceiling, poinsettias and weird vines creeping around the corners, all of them superheated and lovingly sprayed three times a day by Sheena, prioress of the jungle. Well, you don't really have to push your way through the undergrowth to find her desk, but I always felt like I had. And as I sunk into the humid embrace of Naugahyde, I always had the urge to mop my neck with my handkerchief and call her "old girl."

But I never did. Bridget just didn't look that much like Katharine Hepburn, and she wouldn't have got it anyway. I think.

"So," I smiled at her. "Phil looks healthy this morning."

Old Phil is the ony plant I've ever gotten to know by name. He dates from Martin O'Toole's time in that office, and he's an aging philodendron camped out in a cracked pot. He leaks on the carpet when you water him, and he has five big, splayed leaves drooping like the faces of idiot sheep dogs over the arm of the sofa. A very tired vegetable. I like him.

Bridget smiled back and folded her hands on the desk. They looked like two dumplings making love on a railroad tie. "Harry," she began, "I *really* wonder if we shouldn't at least consult with the police about poor Fred."

My pal Fred had become, I guessed forever, "poor Fred" in everybody's mind. So much for the tropical plant chitchat. My employer had a point to make, and she couldn't wait to make it.

"What's on your mind, Bridget? You said something about poor Fred's car." (So I'm snotty—sue me.)

Bridget didn't notice. "There's only one reason Fred was found so soon, Harry. Goodness knows, I don't know as much about this sort of thing as you do. But doesn't it seem that leaving a corpse in a car, in a terrible winter like this one, would be an almost ideal way of confusing a coroner? Why, it—or, rather he—could be there for days before he was found, frozen solid, and how could the time of death ever be determined? Isn't that right?

With superhuman restraint, I did not nod and chant, "Yes, 'Ster." Instead I laughed and lit a cigarette.

"Sure it's right, Bridget. And it's also right—what you're really getting at—that whoever killed Fred must've turned the car lights on after poor Fred was sliced just so he *would* be found this morning. It's a natural. Half the people in the world, probably, will check a parked car with its lights on to see if they can turn 'em off. And one of those was bound to glance back and see the mess in the rear seat. I thought of all that as soon as you told me the tale this morning. So you think you know something the cops don't? The killer wanted the time of death fixed at early this morning. But, hell, if you and I can guess that, why can't the cops?"

I was really enjoying myself—a chance to show her what the real professionals thought like, and how fast they did it. I waited for the smiling cantaloupe to deflate. But it didn't. It smiled harder, with just a touch of patience.

"Good, Harry! I *knew* you'd see the point of leaving the lights on. Father always said you were his brightest young man. But you see, what I think we should consider is the car itself. You follow, don't you?"

I've never been able to say "Aargh!" the way they do in the comics, so I didn't try now. Instead I said, as calmly as I could, "Bridget, I don't even know what you're talking about."

She beamed. She was going to get to demonstrate Pythagoras's theorem to the class dunce all over again. "Harry, the *car!*" she sang. "It was *poor Fred's* car!"

I was beginning to get a headache. "Right. It was poor Fred's car, and poor Fred was in the back of his poor car, chopped into sashimi, when some other poor sucker tried to turn off his headlights and had the crummy luck to look in the back seat. So where else *would* poor Fred be?" I coughed. I smoke too much. Especially at the office.

• *12*

"Why, dear," she said, disappointed, after I'd finished choking, "in the car where he was murdered."

I almost made it this time. Saying "Aargh!" I mean.

"Jesus Harold Christ, Bridget! How the hell do you know Fred didn't buy it in his own car?"

"Oh!" she winced, and blushed. No, not because I'd taken you-know-whose name in vain, but because I must've just said something stupid and she was trying to think of a way of not letting on how dumb it was. "Oh. Well, you see, I don't think poor Fred *could* have been killed in his own car. The reports were explicit, you know, about how—well, how very much he'd been cut up. And that suggests some kind of power tool, doesn't it?"

"Why? Why not a very strong guy with a big, scalpel-sharp something or other?" When I'm being dumb, I don't give it up easy; it's one of my best points.

"No, no, I don't think so. You see, I worked for a while as a surgical nurse—oh, it was years ago, in an Appalachian mission. Oh, my, I haven't thought of that in years. Well," she said, shaking herself out of a reverie I was sorry to see go—it almost made her face look pretty. "Well, you see, I've had to help doctors cut through bone and sinew. And really, Harry, it's *awfully* hard to do by hand. Unless it was someone quite exceptionally strong, it just couldn't be done, or at least not done as thoroughly as this seems to have been done. And, then, whoever was planning to do something like this would have had to have thought things out, and would have come prepared, don't you think?"

I stared. Well, how often do *you* meet retired Mother Superiors who are experts on dismemberment? "Carry on," I grunted.

"Well, yes," she smiled. "Yes. So, how do you run power tools? On gasoline and on electric current. Now gasoline-powered saws are very clumsy and very, very noisy. So unless the killer wanted to attract attention, obviously he or she would use an electric saw."

"Off the car battery," I aarghed. Exactly.

"Exactly! It's very easy to rig with jumper cables. You just have to remember to keep the motor running. And you can even drill holes through the floorboards and run the cables *inside* the car so that you can operate the machine without ever having to get out." (How had she known *that*? Who wanted to ask?)

"Right," I said, "and it only makes sense that whoever cut Fred would do it in his own car instead of Fred's, and risk being seen tapping jumpers on Fred's battery." Despite myself, I was getting interested in this.

"Oh, good, Harry! I was hoping you'd agree!" Agree? Agree to what? "It's just Occam's razor, you know."

"Aargh?"

"Oh, *you* know. William of Occam, late scholastic philosopher. Fourteenth century, if I remember, who said that when you have a number of possible explanations for an event, the simplest and most straightforward is usually the correct one."

"Oh yes, of *course!* How could I have forgotten? Occam's electric buzz saw, and it cut the hell out of Fred Healey. But, Bridget, I still don't see a reason to call the cops on this. You're probably right about everything. All right, dammit, you *are* right about everything," I admitted, catching a glimpse of her sad face. "But aren't the cops going to piece this all together, too? They'll know before we call them that they have to look for a car with a lot of bloodstains and holes in the floorboard. Fine. But it still doesn't get us any closer to knowing why Fred bought it, does it?"

The cantaloupe finally fell. "No. You're right," she sighed. "It only tells us that the killer was known to Fred, has an alibi for last night and this morning, and didn't really dislike poor Fred. Not much to go on, is it?"

Enough, I always say, is enough. Even Phil the philodendron looked sadder than usual at this last show-off of intuition, and I just didn't need any more. "Dammit, Bridget!" I blew up. "That's just *silly,* and you bloody well ought to know that it is. Look, if you want to pester the cops with a bunch of Agatha Christie cufflinks-in-the-soup horseshit deductions, you go right ahead and do it. Me, I've got business to take care of—the business of *this* business, if you remember. And I also have to meet Marianne Healey here in a half hour. So do what you want to do, O.K.? But leave me, and for crying out loud leave the *agency,* out of it."

I try to be a nice man, honest. I don't shout at people and I never take up two parking spaces when I can fit into one. I would buy UNICEF Christmas cards if I had enough people to send a whole box to. But there was Bridget, not saying a word, her hands still folded, making me feel like first runner-up in the Mister America Rat Pageant.

"Certainly, Harry. I'm sorry I bothered you. I'll do what I think best, of course. Talk to you later."

Tough guy that I am, I swaggered back through the undergrowth without even a "be seeing you." Back in my office—just next door to the veldt, but a planet away in spirit and style—I thumbed through the files to date of the three stooges I was to see later: three lives spied upon, surveyed, photographed, boiled down to the shabby details of addresses, times of day, and corespondents. Mr. Brown was definitely getting laid on the side (the South Side, to be precise); Mr. Gray probably wasn't but had a really grade-A paranoid for a wife; and Mrs. Wysocki was playing enough afternoon games for a full basketball season. What a world, what a world, as the Wicked Witch of the West said while she was melting.

I got so engrossed in this uplifting stuff that I didn't notice the time. But at twelve-thirty my phone buzzed again. It was Brenda at the front desk.

"Uh, Harry, Mrs. Healey is here. Can you come get her?" Brenda is all class.

"No, Brenda," I answered. "Just tell her to come on down the hall. She knows the way."

I hung up and lit a cigarette. At the third puff, the door opened and Marianne came in.

It was cold as hell outside and she was wearing a superfuzzy fur coat—one of those artificial things that looks like it's the skin of a peroxide leopard—and underneath it only a black blouse, unbuttoned at the top, and black jeans close-fitting enough to make her mourning, if there was any, become electric.

I got up. Gave her the biggest hug I could manage.

"Marianne," I said. "Sit down, kid. What can I do to help?"

She didn't look like she'd been crying. But her hands shook as she took the cigarette I offered her.

"Harry, I had to see you. I don't know—" she stopped, choking on what she had to say.

I reached across the desk and took her hand. "Ok, Marianne. Take it easy. Now, what is it?"

She took another drag on her smoke, shook back her hair, and smiled. It was the kind of smile you see on people when they hear their cat died.

"Harry, I—I think I killed Fred."

• 4

DID I mention that we were lovers?

Nothing too serious, mind you. But nothing not too serious, either. We were a lot more than just a casual lay to one another, that is. Lovers. We'd met after she married Fred—dinner at Fred's house, in fact. Things had followed things (they often do), and occasionally we were getting together for the odd afternoon delight, even sometimes overnight when Fred was out of town on business. Come to think of it, that was about the time I'd stopped seeing Fred for the occasional after-work beer.

Guilty I'd never really felt. I'd told myself it was a kind of birth defect—you know, like people born without arms never really miss them. I'd never really been able to muster guilt about that sort of thing. But now, while my off-and-on bed buddy sat telling me she was involved in the death of her husband, my friend, I was beginning to imagine how it might feel.

"Marianne," I said. "Honey. Breathe deep, and slow down. Now don't say *anything* to me until you've thought it all out. O.K.?" She nodded. She still had that death's head smile.

"I mean I *killed* him, Harry. When the police came to my— our—house this morning, I already knew he was dead. I knew he had been murdered, because I knew he was *going* to be murdered. The policeman thought I was in shock. Maybe—" she laughed. It wasn't a nice laugh. "Maybe I was. Maybe I still am. I thought I could carry it through, but now I know I can't. I really can't. You have to help me tell them, Harry. I know you will, I know you'll help, because—well."

Saying it all obviously made her feel better. I can't say it did a whole hell of a lot for me, though.

I have one of those little, college dorm refrigerators in my office, and it always has a couple of six-packs of ale nesting in it.

The ale is to wash down the doughnuts, most days. Today I hoped it could wash down a little more.

She shook her head when I offered her one. I didn't speak till I'd taken a long pull.

"Right. You're about to jump out of your skin, you've had a hell of a morning, and you ought to be home asleep with tranqs to the gills. Where's Fred, Jr., by the way?"

"Oh. Oh, a neighbor is watching him. I had to get out of the house, Harry. Reporters have been calling all day."

"Well, for Christ's sake, don't tell them what you just told me. You say you knew Fred would be killed. You didn't hire somebody to do it, did you?"

"Harry! *No*! I didn't—I—I *loved* him!"

It was the first time she'd said that to me.

"No. *No*," she repeated. "We've been having, well, trouble lately. I think he was suspecting—you know." She looked up at me, and I looked at the refrigerator. I'd never thought of myself as "well, *you* know." Yessir, today was going to take some washing down.

"Anyhow," she went on, "last night we had a terrible fight, just before he had to go out. You know how gentle he always was, Harry." I think she blushed. I know I did. "Well, last night he called me things—things—oh, Harry, I couldn't believe it was *him* saying those things!"

She covered her face and sobbed. I sat and folded and refolded my aluminum flip-top till it cracked, and she stopped. I'm not trained as a therapist, and I hate it when people start showing me their scars.

"Well," she sniffled. "He sort of calmed down by the time he left, but we could barely speak to each other." She gazed somewhere I couldn't see.

"And then, he couldn't have been gone more than a half hour, somebody called asking for him. He—whoever it was—said it wasn't important to find him. And Fred always said, never tell anyone where he was when he was working."

"That's the first rule, kid," I grunted. The last thing you want when you're tailing or snooping is a surprise visitor. They're very hazardous to your cover—not to say your health. "You say it was a *he*?"

"Yes, I think so," she sniffed. "It was a kind of high voice—you know, like an alto? But I'm pretty sure it was a man."

"And?"

"And so, I know it's the first rule. But Fred *always* told me where he'd be. Even after—even after last night."

"So you told."

"Yes! Yes! I told! I was so angry, Harry—so hurt. I don't know—maybe I was so hurt because Fred was right about me. Anyway, I thought, well, let somebody ruin one of his damned assignments for once. I hoped it would blow his whole job up in his face. I hoped he would get in big trouble with Northshore, I hoped . . . I hoped I don't know what. Could I have a drink, please?"

I fetched her one, and another for me. She stared at it, but didn't drink. "And then," she went on, "after I'd hung up, I realized I might have gotten him in *real* trouble. And I *did*, I *did*, Harry. I killed him."

She didn't sob this time. She just stared at me with large, dark, dry eyes—eyes that I knew well, that had smiled at me from a lot of rented pillows and gazed at me, with calculated nonchalance, whenever we'd met in Fred's presence. I'd rather she had sobbed.

"Marianne," I said, "didn't you think about warning Fred, after you'd hung up?"

"Of *course* I did! That's *all* I thought about! But there's only a couple of pay phones in the CTA lot, and how could he hear those? So what should I do, drive there to warn him? And what if it *was* just somebody with some kind of news for him? Then I'd look silly for telling, and then telling Fred I'd told. God—I can't even talk straight. Do you see what I mean?"

I saw what she meant. During my own brief disaster of a marriage—I thought of it as my own personal six-day war—I'd learned a lot about the goofy psychology of fighting with somebody you love, how you try and hurt but not hurt too much, and how you never get it quite right.

"Sure," I said. "So you worried yourself sick all night long, and when the cops rang your bell this morning, you knew what they had to tell you, just like a nightmare come true. Jesus, you poor kid."

She got out the first two syllables of "Exactly." And then she did begin sobbing again.

I knew what I was going to do, and I didn't like it one bit. But my weeping friend was in more trouble then she knew. Any cop will tell you that in a homicide investigation, the victim's immediate family are always prime suspects. People like to kill people they *know*. But what he won't tell you is that there are ways of making prime suspects a little more than prime suspects. Ways, I mean, of getting your collar and even getting an indictment where it's easiest to find them. Do *you* know anybody you've really loved that you haven't, one time or another, imagined dead? And if that person *was* dead, would you really feel totally innocent? Cops know the answers to those questions, and they *use* them.

Not that it's even conscious or deliberate, most of the time. You just naturally tend to see what you expect, or hope, to see. What had Bridget O'Toole called it? Occam's razor. The principle of the simplest explanation being the best, the real explanation. Well, that was fine for a class in freshman logic. I'd seen Occam's razor at work for a lot of years, and I knew that it usually cut very dull, with lots of bleeding.

Marianne was still covering her eyes. I rapped with my fist on my desk to get her to raise her eyes. "O.K., kid," I said. "As soon as you get a grip on yourself you're going to realize that none of this—*none* of this, Marianne—is your fault." She started to gulp something. "No! Shut up and listen, dammit! You're half in shock and I'm sorry to act like a bastard, but we haven't got the time for all this. Now. You didn't tell the cops about the call last night?"

"Harry, I *couldn't*. I was frightened, and I felt so guilty. If I hadn't been such a—such a bitch, Fred would still . . ."

"*Genug, schoen*. What I'm telling you, honey, is that you'd better *not* tell them anything now. You know, of course, that you've probably been tailed here."

"Oh, no, I couldn't have been," she gasped. "I mean, I talked to the police this morning and they said they'd get in touch with me when I wanted to talk to them." The innocence of civilians is a continual source of wonder and amusement to me.

"All right, Marianne, whatever you say. But anyhow, it's not going to make any sense, whenever you talk to them, to tell the cops about the phone call. You *don't* have any idea who it might have been, do you?"

"No, no. As I said, I think it was a man—I'm sure it was a man. But it wasn't a voice I recognized."

"Fine. So there's no need to bring it up with the cops. Look—they're going to be working their butts off to find the killer as it is, and if you go to them with this story, all you're going to do is draw them off the track, draw attention to yourself. And, kid, you don't need that." I didn't mention that she might also draw attention to *us*, because that wasn't really part of my worry. I think.

"Harry, are you sure? It seems—I don't know—wrong."

Professor Garnish gave his lecture on ethics. "It isn't, believe me. There's no need to put yourself, and Fred, Jr., through a lot of useless crap. Uh, you haven't mentioned this to anybody else, have you?" She shook her head and my blood pressure went down. "Fine. Now go home. Disconnect the phone. Tell any reporters around the place to bugger off. And sleep."

"No. I can't. I have to go to Calloran's and arrange for the funeral. Oh, Harry, are you sure about all this? It means so much. You *don't* think it's my fault?"

"Kid, kid, kid. You don't even know that the guy who called you had anything to do with it. In fact, he probably didn't. Would *you* call somebody and risk being identified on the phone if you were about to—you know?"

Her face brightened a little. Just a little, but it was worth it. "Why, no, I wouldn't!" Bullshit works wonders, especially with the bereaved.

I gave her another hug and a chaste kiss and told her I'd see her out. It was early afternoon but I felt like I'd been in the office for a week. Obstructing justice, even for a friend, makes the room stuffy.

I told Brenda I'd be back in a few minutes, and we walked into the frigid sunshine. O'Toole Investigations shares a single-story building with Miss Kathy's Academy of Dance—one big room, thirty folding chairs, and a forty-five RPM record player—and Ben Gross Dry Cleaners. I've never met Miss Kathy. But Ben, with an endless supply of dried smoked herring and a complete edition of Dickens in the shop, and with a number on his arm

(Treblinka), is a good friend. He taught me to say things like *"genug, schoen,"* among much else. I waved at his crinkled, dried-apple little face as we passed his window.

The air was minus fifteen, at least, with the windchill, and it felt great. Marianne leaned against me as we walked to her car and, dammit, that felt good too. Now we had a *nasty* little secret between us, and it was like a new level of intimacy: risky, maybe even harmful, but somehow exciting. Rat that I am, I even began to wonder, as she fished in her purse for her keys, how long she would think a proper period of mourning would be.

And then two things happened. I spotted an Evanston P.D. car parked across the street, a little down the block. The cops in it weren't looking at us, and I had the feeling that they weren't looking at us on purpose.

Then Marianne groaned and leaned harder against me. For a second I thought she'd seen the police car, too. But she leaned harder than *that*, and as she slumped in my arms I saw the blood staining the front of her blonde, artificial fur coat.

• 5

THE cops saw it at almost the same time I did, and were out of their car and halfway across the street before I could holler for them.

"She's been shot!" I said as they came up to me. Marianne's blood was trickling off my sleeve by now, onto the ice of the parking lot. It looked like a lot of blood. "Get an ambulance, for Chrissake!" I was kneeling, cradling her in my lap. Her eyes were open, but she was staring at nothing, not making a sound.

"Right!" snapped the shorter of the two cops, who turned on his heel and sprinted back to his car. The other cop I knew: Patrolman Al Caceres, two-hundred-fifty pounds, at least three pounds of it mustache, smart as hell, and able to mangle anybody slow enough for him to catch. A Puerto Rican walrus in a too small uniform, and right then, he looked beautiful.

"Al," I said. "Did you see anything?"

"Fucking *nada*," he grumbled. As he spoke, panting like a kerosene engine and billowing steam into the cold air, he took Marianne off my lap—gently, gently, like a nurse or a mother— laid her on the ground, and shrugged his coat off to cover her. It would have covered three of her.

"Didn't see shit, didn't hear shit," he growled again, smoothing back her hair and wincing as she moaned. Al hated to see people get hurt unless he'd decided they needed hurting. He's a *good* cop.

"Must've been somebody in one of them goddam buildings," he continued, glaring at the office buildings, service stations, and banks up and down the street. "And by the looks of the wound, must've been some sonofabitch with a *cannon*. I think she'll make it, though—lucky, but it looks like the bastard caught the shoulder."

I agreed. It was a big wound, and a lot of blood, but Marianne, though in shock, was still there and still breathing. If I judged the position of the wound right through her coat, though, a few inches farther up and she wouldn't have been lucky. There would have been more hole than head.

"The ambulance'll be right here," gasped the short cop, running back from the patrol car. He looked inquiringly at Al, got a nod and a wink, and trotted off again to check the buildings. Lotsa luck: Al was too old and too smart to go on a fool's errand himself. He looked up at me.

"O.K., Harry. I guess you know why we were here to begin with. Got anything you want to tell me, or do you want to save it for Inspector Carp?"

Inspector Carp is in charge of CAP—Crimes Against Persons—for the Village of Skokie, where Fred had been killed. I don't see him often and whenever I do, I'm happy I don't. Al Caceres, as an officer for a neighboring township, sees him a lot more than I do and likes it even less.

"Al," I said, "if I had anything to tell, believe me, I'd tell *you*. She came to see me because, you know, Fred and I go way back. I guess she just needed to get away from everything, just wanted to talk to somebody—anybody. But no, she didn't really say anything, just sobbed a lot."

Al looked at me oddly. Then he sighed. "Sure, Harry, you oughta know the rules of the game by now. But don't be surprised if Carp asks you for a dance sometime soon. Jesus, where's the goddam *ambulance*?" he shouted. Al's a *very* good cop.

"Oh, no—how awful. Mr. Caceres, how is she? Harry, what happened?"

Right—it was Bridget O'Toole. The inevitable, gawking, and obstructing crowd had begun to gather (where do those people *come* from?), and Bridget, somehow, had pushed her way through it—coatless, but showing no sign of shivering.

Al grunted a respectful hello. I walked her back towards the office, explaining briefly what was going on, and not mentioning, of course, the phone call Marianne had received the night before. The ambulance arrived, the backup car arrived, and two more cops got out of it and began checking the neighborhood. And Al stood there as they drove Marianne away, waiting for me to ride back to the station with him.

As I left her at the door, Bridget glared at me. "You know what this means, of course," she said.

"No, what—war?" I mocked.

But she really was angry. "Stop it!" she barked. "Your friend, *Father's* friend, is dead, and his wife has just been shot right outside our door. Enough is enough, Harry. Like it or not, we have to do something to help. You owe it, you know, if not to Fred, at least to Marianne."

I would have stared, but I didn't have the time. Caceres was waiting. Christ, did she *know*? Well, anyway, I felt Sister Mary Vengeance blocking the door, clouding the air, and clenching her fists, with what I tried to make a very noncommital nod and grimace.

The Evanston Police Headquarters is on Grove and Asbury, which is only about a mile-and-a-half from our office. That may excuse the fact that I was inside their front door before I remembered.

"Oh, *shit!*" I said eloquently as Al and I entered. "Marianne's kid is with a babysitter. Somebody had better see to him."

But Al was ahead of me (surprise, surprise). "Not a babysitter, man, a neighbor. Mrs. Girard. We got a guy on his way out there now. Mrs. G. don't have any kids of her own, so she'll probably spring for watching the kid—at least tonight."

Sometimes you almost think there *is* an Officer Friendly. Still, I was worried about Fred, Jr. I'd spent a lot of time playing with the boy, and I liked him. So Al, after delivering me to the interrogation room, went to check with child care to make sure he would be looked after.

I got out of the Evanston Police Headquarters an hour later, little the worse for wear, about four o'clock in the afternoon. I'd said nothing beyond what I'd told Caceres, and they had nothing, really, to ask me. Still, I had to tell them nothing three times before they were satisfied. They're like that. Fortunately Inspector Carp, king of the pig people, was still, as far as anybody knew, feeding his pet weasel in Skokie. His Evanston counterpart, Detective Brutelle, was a nice little guy who used too much shaving lotion and who didn't seem to know why I was there at all, except to be asked to tell the same boring story three times in a row and dismissed, with advice not to leave Cook County.

By the time I left, though, a couple of items had come in, which

Brutelle was happy to share with me. A thorough search of the area had turned up nothing that might indicate who shot Marianne. And Marianne would be all right. It was "only a flesh wound," as those silly bastards who have never *had* a flesh wound describe it, and therefore don't know that when you're talking about firing a shell into a living body, there's no such word as "only."

Al Caceres drove me back to the office to pick up my car.

"You going back to work?" he asked when he pulled into the lot. He looked straight ahead, unconcerned, as he asked. I didn't buy it.

"No, old buddy, I'm not going back to work." I lit a cigarette in my best nonchalant style. It never fools anybody. "I'm going to check on Fred, Jr. at the address you so kindly gave me, and see if there's anything I can do there. Then I'm going to Evanston Hospital to check on Mar—on Mrs. Healey. And then I'm going home to a TV dinner. If you feel like tailing me, you might as well meet me at my place to eat. It's tacos and refried beans tonight, and I think there's some beer in the ice box."

"Hey, *amigo*," Al laughed, and grinned at me. With an accent about as exotic as Dan Rather's, he only lapses into Spanish when he's (a) excited, or (b) pulling your chain. He was not excited. "Listen, man"—he pronounced it *mahn*—"I'm off duty in an hour, and I got *my own* plans for tonight, you know?" I didn't, and I didn't care, but I nodded like I did—always humor a cop. "I just wondered what you were doing."

"And I just told you what I'm doing, *amigo*," I said. "Listen, Al, I know you're a good guy. We've shot enough pool and drunk enough booze for me to know you wouldn't fuck me over unless you had to, O.K.? But you're a cop—a good cop—and you know, and I know, that that means you or somebody is going to be on my ass for a while. Because Fred Healey was my friend. And because Fred Healey's wife was shot while she was visiting me. And because," I sighed, "because you probably know a few other things I wish you didn't." That was a stupid thing to say, but I was tired.

Al grinned harder. No, really, *harder.*

"Garnish, you're the funniest guy I know. Honest, you break me up. You think you're a suspect because you've been sleeping with Healey's wife? *Hell,* man, *everybody* knows that!"

Wonderful, isn't it, to be a master of detection and concealment.

"No, listen," he continued, "I don't want to be a bastard like that *maricon* Carp, but the lady's getting shot right next to you is a piece of luck for *you,* you know? We know you're too sharp— and too poor—to hire a mechanic to set something like that up, and it really lets you off the hook for Healey's thing. Now," and he shifted his great bulk toward me, "now I ain't saying you ain't the first guy *some* guys thought of for the collar. But not now. Relax, man, you're *clean!*"

"Ah, darling, you make me feel so safe," I sighed. He laughed, I laughed, and I walked to my car. I walked slowly, not looking back; I wanted to give my pal enough time to call in the tail on me before I drove out of the lot. Why fight city hall? They couldn't be more than a block or so away, anyhow, having followed us from the station.

Fred lived—*had* lived—on Western, just over the Evanston border into Chicago. It's a nice area, where the houses are still suburban-looking, but where the city makes itself felt in things like more bars per square mile, narrower streets, heavier traffic, and a higher mugging rate. Mrs. Girard, Fred's babysitter, lived in a frame house that hadn't been painted in years, just two doors down from the Healey house, which hadn't been painted in years.

Mrs. Girard opened the door in a housecoat thrown over a sweatshirt and denim shorts, and a pair of fuzzy slippers that looked like they'd been swimming recently. Mrs. Girard exhaled the unmistakable odor of juniper berries. She was a very sexy drunk, but I was bothered at the thought of her minding the kid.

She slurred a few sympathetic, isn't-it-terrible clucks as she led me into the house. She had told the police that she would take care of young Fred for as long as need be (neither Fred nor Marianne had any family to speak of who were still living in the area).

"We don't have any of our own, you know, so it'll be kind of fun," she said. "Bill, my husband, works the night shift, so I can really use the company, you know?"

She smiled up at me—and I'm not that tall—a little, sad, boozy, friendly woman. Her eyes were on the point of being moist. Suddenly I felt easier about the idea of leaving the boy with her.

Fred, Jr. was sitting on the floor of the den, his back against a daybed, watching a cartoon cat attack a cartoon mouse on television. He was clutching a big stuffed panda bear, with tacking leaking out of its left shoulder.

Marianne had been shot in the right.

I had given Fred the panda for his fourth birthday, last year. It was named Arnold.

"Hey, Freddie," I tried to chirp. "How're you and old Arnold here doing?"

Fred has pale blue eyes, like me, a trait the biologists call "recessive," which means that if you mate blue-eyed genes with brown-eyed genes, the brown, on the average, win out and you get brown-eyed kids. Marianne and the kid's father of record both had brown eyes. It was another reason for buying teddy bears. He turned his bothersome blue eyes on me.

"Arnold got hurt," he said, and held the leaking shoulder up for me to inspect. "Daddy got hurt, too, today. And mommy's not coming home tonight. Miz Girard says I'll stay here." He watched me try to close Arnold's wound.

"Uncle Harry, I don't *want* to stay here."

Uncle Harry explained how it would be best for him to stay there, how his mommy was feeling bad and couldn't take care of him today, how Miz Girard was a really super, nice lady, and how Uncle Harry would be back tomorrow to check on him, maybe even take him out to a movie or something. Would he like to see *Star Wars* again? Uncle Harry could tell he wasn't doing a damned bit of good.

"By the way, buddy, what happened to poor Arnold?" I don't react to pain as well as, say, Al Caceres.

The boy's eyes got wider. "I did it, this morning. If daddy's hurt, then Arnold's hurt too. Do you think he'll get better?"

Assuming he meant the bear, I told him of course—it would be easy to fix. It would be easy to fix. I kissed him on the forehead and left him watching television. The tables had turned, and now the mouse was annihilating the cat. But maybe it was a different cartoon.

• 6

THAT was Friday. I spent Friday night at the hospital. Marianne couldn't see anybody yet, the young doctor on her case advised me, but she was doing very well, indeed—was a very lucky woman—I could talk to her tomorrow. And tapped his clipboard (interview over) and quickstepped on down the hall. I stayed till two in the morning anyhow, drinking coffee and reading the same issue of *Newsweek* five times, cover to cover.

Saturday and Sunday I helped arrange for Fred's funeral—they would plant him Monday morning—seeing the priest at St. Polycarp's about the mass, making sure Mrs. Girard (still in sweatshirt and shorts, but sober, and still sexy) had everything she needed for the boy. And visiting Marianne.

We didn't talk about the shooting, or about Fred. We didn't talk much about anything, just sat there and stared at the television, the walls, the flowers (Bridget had sent flowers). She was to be released late Sunday, and by noon Sunday, Fred, Jr. had gotten the news—all the news—and Marianne's mother had flown in from Santa Barbara, where she'd gone after her divorce, to take charge of things. (The father had blown his head off, for no apparent reason, six years ago, and the liquor stores, part of the settlement, had been keeping the mother in suntan oil out in lotusland.) I dropped Marianne at her home Sunday, but didn't go in.

All that weekend, at the hospital, at St. Polycarp's, at Calloran's Funeral Home, I kept running into my softhearted boss. Bridget would fuss over Marianne, fuss over the arrangements for the mass, fuss over me—over, in fact, anybody who got within fussing range. She was in one of those moods where she's like a condolence card searching for an appropriate disaster.

And every time I ran across her we had the same conversation.

She wanted to "do something" about Fred and Marianne. I kept telling her that there was nothing to "do," that we had less to work with than the police, and that anyhow we weren't—fiction notwithstanding—crimestoppers. We were hired snitches, sneaky little elves armed with Polaroids working for dirty people with grudges. And we had best stay as far out of the whole thing as we could. God knew we were already in it more than was good for us. None of it made much of an impression, as you'll see, on either of us.

And then Monday, the day of the funeral, I got a special delivery.

The alarm went off at eight-thirty. I made coffee, poached an egg, and turned on the tube just in time to catch Sylvester and Tweety. Tweety had swallowed some mad scientist's formula, and was turning into a monster canary, beating the crap out of Sylvester. The poor cat couldn't figure out why his whole world had turned ugly and was out to get him.

Well, things were tough all over and getting tougher. It was time to head for Calloran's, and the funeral.

Ben Gross tells me that the custom with the Jewish dead is to get them to hell underground before the next sunset after they die. And having gone to enough Chicago Catholic funerals, I can see how smart that is. Because what *we* do, you see, is to stretch the whole damned thing out until everybody is about as tired and stiff from the whole thing as the corpse himself. All that crap you've heard about Irish wakes, in other words, is just that: crap. People come, people go, sign the register, and stand around talking in voices about ten decibels lower than they normally use, or than can be heard, and feel uncomfortable, and wish they were the hell out of the funeral parlor watching Monday night football. "*Nu,* Harry," says Ben, pouring tea (one of these days I'll probably figure out what *nu* means). "*Nu,* Harry. Why do you people like to linger so much about what doesn't do anybody any good?"

I just sit there and sip my tea (I don't like tea) and tell him I'm not Irish, I'm Czech. He never really believes me.

Anyhow, Calloran's funeral home is on Skokie Boulevard, one of the main drags in town since it leads right to Old Orchard, the *big* shopping center. Mike Calloran, who runs the place, is very big around the North Shore. He throws money at his parish like he was running for something. But he's not; he just wants to make sure that when mommy or daddy or Uncle Max kicks off and you find yourself numb from grief and at the same time worried about casket costs and burial arrangements and time of day for the requiem mass, you think of Mike.

He's very good at his work.

He doesn't even look like an undertaker (I think they prefer another word, anyhow). Undertakers are supposed to be long, tall, and solemn. Mike Calloran looks like a fuzzy tomato in a blue serge suit; his face is always flushed, his blonde hair is always trying to explode out of his head, and he's one of those Irishmen who can't seem to stop smiling.

He was smiling as I filed into the room for the short prayers before we carted Fred off to church. But not at me. The judge, Gerald Solomon (you'll hear more about him later), had just bumbled in. And when the Judge bumbles anywhere, people start talking to him. He was an old friend and patron of Fred's, and one sign of how fond he must have been of Fred was that he pried himself loose from the bar he ran to go to the funeral at all. Normally, the Judge is never seen out of his bar.

Which is why, I guess, Mike Calloran was falling all over himself to make the Judge feel welcome. I was just as happy not to be noticed.

Father MacMahon hadn't arrived yet to start the prayers, so people were standing around feeling silly about being dressed up that early in the morning. There weren't many. Bridget, of course, plumped down moist-eyed on one of the folding chairs along the wall. As I came in she smiled at me and patted the chair beside her and I pretended not to notice. Marianne, just out of the hospital, to whom I walked up and gave a consoling hug and said some suitably dumb things, looked pale and scared and, I thought, eminently ready to be taken to bed. Good man, Garnish, I thought. At the poor bastard's wake, you're getting horny for his widow. Well, I never said I was a nice man, did I, now?

Besides Bridget and Marianne, there were a few guys I recognized from Northshore, Inc., though I didn't see Ed Brady. Ed was the president of Northshore and, by everything I'd heard, the richest and most successful private detective in the whole damn frozen city of Chicago. I supposed he had better things to do—a round of golf, say, in a heated sportsdome—and anyway, the company had sent flowers.

There was Mrs. Girard, looking considerably less sexy in a black dress than she did in her houseclothes, minding Fred, Jr., who was in a cute little suit, and who didn't really seem to know what was going on. Lucky Fred, Jr. After I had hugged and stupid-remarked to Marianne, I crossed over to them, said what I hoped were some kind things to Mrs. Girard, and asked Fred, Jr. how Arnold the bear was doing.

Arnold Bear, Fred, Jr. told me, had died during the night. Terrific.

And there was one other guy I couldn't place, a short, skinny guy with unruly red hair. He must be another of Fred's friends from Northshore, I thought.

Just as Bridget had decided I wasn't going to notice her, and was sailing toward me full of goodwill and condolence, I got lucky and Father MacMahon came in. Everybody shuffled to a kind of religious attention—except the little red-haired man, who kept his seat, and Fred, Jr., who had decided to try and find bees in the flowers around his daddy's casket. But Bridget stopped in mid-course and, like a sunflower, turned to bask in Father's presence. Conditioning works, you know? It's like all those ex-cons who still pace out the dimensions of their cells, or ex-GI's who have to restrain the urge to salute officers on the street.

Father MacMahon, a silver-haired good-looker who had seen one Pat O'Brien movie too many, had a warm smile and a warm word for everybody. Mike Calloran discreetly moved to the back of the room, MacMahon positioned himself in front of the casket, said a few kind things (I wondered how many times he's said the same kind things—it was the religious version of instant coffee), and began the prayers: a Hail Mary, and an our Father, and a hearty "Let the Perpetual Light Shine Upon Him," and we moved out.

There were only four pallbearers. Usually there are six, but I suppose Fred couldn't muster that many friends, or maybe Marianne didn't know that many of Fred's friends. Me, and three guys from Northshore.

And as we were loading the casket into the back of the hearse, I got my special delivery.

Mike Calloran and two of his assistants—tall, grey men—were getting the casket into the hearse while the official pallbearers stood around shivering and feeling foolish. Then Mike broke away from his assistants and came over to me, still smiling his ass off.

"Harry Garnish, right?" he said, and held out a gloved hand. I took it and grunted.

"Harry, before we, well, start, I wonder if I could just talk to you for a minute," Calloran said.

We strolled away from the hearse and as we did, Calloran's smile faded. By twenty feet from anybody else, it had become, by God, a real frown. I felt like I was seeing him for the first time.

"Look, Garnish," he said—and even the used car salesman voice had changed into an almost human register—"I don't know what the hell this is all about, but I've got something for you. Healey"—I noticed he was no longer "Fred"—"Healey came to see me a few days ago. He gave me this, and told me if anything happened to him I should deliver it to you." With that, he handed me a brown paper package about the size of a deck of cards. It had my name scrawled on it, with a scrawl I recognized from a hundred office memos and a hundred more dirty jokes left on my desk. It was Fred's handwriting.

"Goddammit, Garnish," Calloran barked as I took it and slipped it into my inside jacket pocket. "I *hate* getting mixed up in shit like this. But I've got a reputation in the community for being trustworthy, so I promised Healey I'd do what he asked. Whatever this means, though, you'd better leave me *out* of it, you hear? And I hope you realize what a risk I took for your friend."

"Right," I said. "I'll tell him what a brave bastard you are when I see him. Or maybe, with luck, you'll see him first." And we strode back to the hearse, where the mourners were staring at us curiously. Except for the little red-haired man who, I noticed, had disappeared.

A requiem mass is one of those occasions where you count the holes in the ceiling tiles, if you're lucky enough to be in a church where they have ceiling tiles with holes in them. Usually, that is.

As I listened to MacMahon drone through the liturgy, I kept feeling for the little packet in my pocket. And we drove from St. Polycarp's to the cemetery, I found it hard to keep up the chitchat with my three pallbearer-buddies. Marianne, of course, cried through the whole thing; so did Mrs. Girard; so did Bridget. I couldn't figure out which of them meant it more.

After the graveside service, and the hugs and kisses, I rode in the hearse back to Calloran's, declined an invitation to the inevitable postfuneral lunch (Mrs. Girard was hosting it, since Marianne had been in the hospital), and drove like hell back to my apartment.

And then I stared at the pacakage for a good half hour before I worked up the nerve to open it. I made coffee, I walked around my three rooms, I flipped the TV on and off, and finally there was nothing to do but check the damned thing out.

It was a cassette tape, of course. And it was officially police property, and I didn't give a damn. My hands were cold, and they were shaking.

I have a tape deck—but, of course, Fred had known, or was it Fred *knew*, that? I thumbed Dizzy Gillespie out of the chamber—sorry, Diz, you've been upstaged—poured myself another cup of coffee, lit a cigarette, and pushed the ON button.

It wasn't only Fred's writing, it was Fred's voice.

"Hi, Harry," said the machine, while I felt the chill move from my hands up my arms to the top of my head. "If you're listening to this, then I'm dead. And you're probably surprised as hell." I swear to God, he *laughed*.

"But relax. If you're hearing this at all, then all that is over and done with. Over and done with. Because I'm dead. Funny to sit here saying that. I. Am. Dead." The tape ran silent for some seconds, and I could almost see Fred shake himself when he began again. "Well. Anyhow. The reason you're getting this tape, pal, is because I want you to do something for me. No, I don't want you to find my killer. That doesn't matter. It'll have been a pro, I think, most likely out-of-state talent, hired by people—by people you couldn't even touch."

Once again I had that sense of my old friend shaking himself out of a reverie.

"No, Harry, what I want you to do is just a kind of messenger service. I want you to get something for me. And then I want you to take that something somewhere, where you will get a lot of money—a *lot* of money, Harry—for it. And then I want you to put the money in a bank, in an account made out to the name of Marianne Healey—you remember her, don't you, Harry?"

I thumbed the tape recorder to OFF and got up to make some more coffee. While I waited for it to perk I paced around the kitchenette, staring at the tape player in the other room like was a snake. It was.

Dammit, if he had *known*, why didn't he just *tell* me he knew? Why didn't he come after me and beat the hell out of me? He was bigger than I was, and we both knew he could. Why pull this suffering-in-silence crap on me—*me*, his best friend—and then, when he knew his back was against the wall, send me *this* ?

If I just reversed the tape to the beginning, carefully rewrapped it, and took it to the police, I told myself, I would be well out of it. Oh, maybe a few more people would learn about me and Marianne. But from what Al Caceres, not to mention Bridget, had said to me, it seemed about as much a secret as the results of the last world series, anyhow—and about as important.

And if I listened to any more of the tape, I told myself, I could wind up being complicit in what so far sounded like a blackmail operation, for the sake of a dead man who already knew what a rat I really was, and for no sake except the sake of a friendship that I'd violated, and that he knew I'd violated.

It's why I hate arguing with myself: I'm such a rat, and know I'm such a rat, that I can't trust my own advice. I poured a cup of coffee that hadn't finished perking, went back to the living room, and pushed the ON button again.

"Sorry to run on like this, Harry," said the voice on the cassette. I think I raised my coffee cup in a silent toast. "It's just that, you know, if you *do* hear this, then I *am* dead, and it's like if I keep talking—even though you hear this after I've bought it— I'll—I'll—I don't know, somehow stay alive a little longer. And, believe me, I know what kinds of problems I'm making for you just by sending you this. But, then, you *do* owe me, don't you?"

The pleasant voice had turned to a snarl, and I thought for a moment of switching the tape off again. But I—Fred—Fred's killer—somebody—had gone too far. I let it run.

"So," said my dead pal. "Remember Ryan's Pub, on Wacker, where we used to have so much fun?" Indeed I did. A hundred drunken Irishmen marching into the place, cardboard green hats held high, demanding, on St. Patrick's Day, after the big parade, instant service, noisily intolerant of those with the bad luck not to be—or not to claim to be—Irish on this splendid day. I was not Irish, nor did I claim to be; Garnish is the anglicized version of a Czechoslovakian name you don't even want to hear. I thought the whole business was a lot of silliness, and had said so frequently to my boss Bridget O'Toole, my ex- and dead friend Fred Healey, and, in short, anyone to whom the expression of such an opinion might be deemed a personal affront. It's just a part of my lifelong scheme of self-preservation, folks.

No time passed between his mention of the place and my memory of it.

"I know you do. Well, old buddy, old pal, what I want you to do is just this. You go to Ryan's Pub on Wacker, and you order a drink and then you go to the can. There's a key taped inside the tank of the can, just above the water line, and the key has a number on it. Take that key to Union Station, and get a package out of the box that has that number on it. It's a very dismal, very small package." He was still the only guy I knew who could use a word like "dismal" and not sound affected.

"Don't try to find out what's in the package," my old, dead friend went on, "because it's not anything you'll understand, even if you try to open the damned thing.

"Now, this is important, old pal, old buddy. Don't screw it up. You take the package to the office of Mister Harmon Wright in the Hancock Building. *Ecology International* is the name on the doors of the offices. Take no crap from whatever secretaries you may run into. Insist on seeing Mister *Wright*. And when you do see him, give him the little package. He'll know what it's all about, what it all means, but don't you let him take too long to look at it or to give you an answer. Be a *prick*, Harry—I know you've got it in you—and don't you walk out of that office with less than twenty thousand dollars in your pocket. And I mean certified checks, man. You take that to whatever bank you choose, and you open an account in Marianne's name, and then when you feel like it you let her know what you did. I figure, you see, that you'll have lots of time to talk."

If the bastard hadn't been dead, I might have found it in me to kill him myself.

"It's not for me, you know," the voice droned on. "And I guess it's not even for Marianne. But it is for young Fred. It's for my son. It's for his education. Funny, you know, Harry? He's the one thing I have left in all this stupidity."

The OFF Button was sitting there, glaring at me with a plastic red eye. But there's a point of no return for everything—lives and cassettes include— and I had passed it. I wished I was dead, and continued to listen.

"Anyhow, don't worry, Harry," said the machine on my coffee table where I have never yet put coffee. "Nobody is going to hurt you over this. And don't take it to the cops. They'll just find the package and drill poor Wright until he calls his White House connections, but he'll never be able to tell them what the hell is going on, and the package won't help them a bit. And, of course, since I'm dead, I'm inadmissable evidence, aren't I?" He seemed to laugh at that. "Yeah, of *course* I'm inadmissable. Even if I *say* that I am. Hey! Jury! Are you there? Look at me, boys and girls, I'm *inadmissable*!

"Just think of this tape as a life insurance policy, Harry. I'm making you the—what's the word?—the beneficiary, no, no, the *executor* of my will because I know you'll do just what I ask, because it's for Marianne and for the kid."

He didn't say "my kid." He said "the kid." It probably meant nothing. As Othello said to Iago. (I hadn't hung around Ben Gross all these years for nothing.)

"Don't worry, Harry. I know how much you hate trouble, and, believe me, nobody is going to hurt you over this. I know you hate getting into trouble, and this is absolutely safe." If it was so absolutely safe, I wondered, why was he repeating himself about my not getting hurt? It was like buying pencils from a blind man: you knew you could cheat him, but you knew that if you *did* cheat him, there wouldn't be anything left worth calling "you".

"I'm taping this on Thursday," Fred's voice went on. "Monday if I'm still here I can destroy it. I hope you never hear this.

But if you do, if you do—well, so long, Harry. You're all right, man, I mean you are one of the people I like best, in spite of—whatever. Funny, isn't it? I can't think of anybody else to send this to. Because I can't think of anybody else I—I *trust*. What do you make of that?

That's all there was. I let the tape hiss on to its end while I got dressed and drank some more coffee. Then I locked the cassette in my desk drawer.

Look at it this way: I'd already obstructed justice once, to protect Fred's widow and my whatever. Why not compound the interest?

And, besides, things were *getting* interesting, in an ominous sort of way. Mr. Harmon Wright, the fellow I was supposed to get the money from for whatever was checked at Union Station, was a very big fish.

Or mammal, to be more accurate.

Ecology International was a very big nonprofit concern dedicated to saving baby harp seals, right whales, snow leopards—all those poor bastards who, I hear, won't be around anyhow come 2000, whatever we try to do, RIP Moby Dick. They printed calendars where the leopards looked sad and the whooping cranes looked endangered, they ran television commercials with plaintive, whale-song soundtracks, and they bankrolled, I had heard, a lot of those guys with lumberjack shirts and love beads who like to stand between Japanese harpooners and their targets.

All very nonprofitmaking and downright upright. But Mr. Harmon Wright, founder and president of E.I., was also one of the wealthiest and most visible men in the city. The money, mainly, was inherited, though young Harmon probably had to be pretty damned good just not to lose the silver platter he'd been handed—the biggest game, after all, draws the most predators—and in fact he had even managed to polish the platter a little. Around 1900, Granddad General Winston Wright had built an empire of grocery stores and canning factories. (I wondered if they sold whale meat?) But young Harmon had diversified and vertically-integrated the hell out of the kingdom transmitted through his father from his grandfather. Beyond a certain level, though, "rich" and "richer" have no real meaning. At least not to those of us looking up from the first floor.

Anyhow, a few years ago Wright announced dramatically that he was stepping out of Wright Industries and devoting full-time energy, and a hell of a lot of money, to "keeping the planet in trust for our children," as he put it. Many people thought it was the first move in a bid for the governorship, or even for the United States Senate. It certainly sounded pretentious enough to qualify for either office. But he appeared really to *believe* in what he was doing. Ecology had suddenly become *the* hip cause in this town. Wright would buy out an evening's tickets for a save-the-snow-leopard gala at the opera, hire big-name rock bands for champagne-and-boogie harp seal disco evenings, and all at a grand a ticket—and he knew the people who could afford it. There probably wasn't a penthouse on Lake Shore Drive that didn't have this year's Ecology International calendar on the wall over the Jacuzzi—$2.50 in the bookstores, but for *you*, $250.00.

And Wright's wife, an ex-model who moved like a snow leopard herself, was filmed inaugurating some humanitarian do or another at least once a month. She'd probably cut more cords than a Calcutta midwife.

So. I had told Bridget O'Toole that we had no business getting mixed up in Fred's murder. I had even half-convinced her, I flattered myself. And in the process of half-convincing her, I had concealed evidence, entered into a conspiracy, and now I was on my way, on a dead man's advice, to blackmail a millionaire humanitarian. The thing I like so much about life is its rationality.

The kicker was, I didn't *care* who killed Fred. And if Harmon Wright was in any way involved in it, I really didn't want to *know*. Friend of the whales or not, he was known to have the self-preservation instincts of a shark, and the clout to back it all up. I didn't share Bridget's goofy sense of justice, or vengeance. I've never been able to tell them apart, sorry.

But there was one thing. There was a lady I'd slept with who had a big gunshot wound in her shoulder. And there was another. There was a kid who'd ripped his favorite bear in some weird voodoo attempt to make his dead daddy well. And there was another. A friend who had died knowing I'd done to him what friends don't do to one another.

It was a debt. To whom, don't ask, because I still don't know.

By twelve o'clock I figured I could start fighting the ice and the traffic down to Ryan's Pub. I had just locked the apartment door behind me when the phone rang. Cursing, I let myself back in and raced for the receiver.

I should have saved the curse. It was my employer. "Harry," said Bridget.

"Bridget," panted Harry.

"Harry, I'm so glad you're at home. You've had two calls at the office since this morning"—my home phone is unlisted—"and they both sound rather urgent. Inspector Carp requests that you come in and see him as soon as you can. Something to do with poor Marianne's shooting, of course."

Of course. I should have known that, sooner or later, I'd wind up facing Carp and having to lie to him. He is a very hard man to lie to.

"O.K.," I sighed. "If he could wait till today to call for me, he can wait till later this afternoon. And the other call, Bridget?"

"Oh, yes. The other call is from a Mrs. Wright, Mrs. Yolanda Wright." She read me a number. "She wouldn't leave a message, and I couldn't find her on our client roster, but she sounded terribly anxious to talk to you. She says she has to talk to you, and today. Oh! Yolanda Wright! Isn't she the wife of Harmon Wright, the millionaire?"

She sure as hell was.

• 7

RYAN's Pub on Wacker is the kind of place that almost renews your faith in cities.

What I hate about this city—and about all cities these days, is the way bars are dying a slow, lingering death or disappearing altogether. They're being strangled to death by "cocktail lounges," and those that aren't strangled only survive by adapting and *becoming* "cocktail lounges." The real bar is—as surely as the right whale or the whooping crane—an endangered species.

Of course, you may not know the difference between a bar and a "cocktail lounge." And if you don't, then you've never been in a real bar, and it's sorry I am for you.

Ryan't Pub, for instance, is a bar. There are no teenage waitresses to hover over your booth, dressed like the ghosts of a Las Vegas chorus line, shaking self-important and overdeveloped tits while they (the waitresses, that is) take your order. What you want to drink you order at the bar, and you carry from the bar. There is no overplush upholstery on the bar seats; you don't sink five inches once you sit down with your drink. Instead, there are benches, good healthy benches made of mere wood, and an archeologist would probably be able to locate some Mayan carvings on them, they are that old and have remained undisturbed for that long. (This has a practical purpose: When you can't read the carvings, or when you can't find a level place for your glass on the carved surfaces, you know you are drunk and should go home.)

Also there is no jukebox, there is no space for a band, there *are* hard boiled eggs (five cents), and it is worth your life if you come in in a three-piece suit and ask for Perrier with a twist of lemon.

I love the place. On St. Patrick's Day it's a haven for the terminally stupid, and most of the rest of the year it's a hangout for the psychological walking wounded. But still, by God, it's a *place*. It feels like a place. It feels different from the space around it—warmer, say, and less hurried. Kindly. I was glad that, whatever else might happen, Fred Healey had chosen this place for me to begin my career as a blackmailer.

I had decided, on the drive down, that whether I called Mrs. or tried to see Mr. Wright first, I had better be sure Fred's goody was safe in my pocket. I'd parked two blocks from Ryan's and walked, or lurched, freezing my tail off, into the wind, toward the bar. The burst of warm, beer-soaked air that surrounded me as I pushed inside, and the low murmur of the four or five people scattered in the place, was like an angel's kiss. I dropped my coat in an empty booth and went to the bar to order an Irish coffee. In Ryan's they serve it in a mug, not a cute little thin-stemmed glass, and they don't have any whipped cream to top it off with, thank God.

I carried my mug into the men's room.

There was only one stall, with a wooden door that might have been old enough to be donated to the Smithsonian. I went in, latched the door (with a leather loop over a nail, for crying out loud), took a gulp of the Irish coffee, and lifted the lid off the tank.

The key wasn't there.

It wasn't taped to the side of the tank, it wasn't taped to the float, it wasn't in the water or wedged in the works. And if the key wasn't there, then—unless Fred Healey was a deathbed liar—then somebody knew it had been there. Somebody who might be waiting for somebody else to come looking for it. I was beginning to sweat. Ryan's Pub was fast losing its old-world charm.

I replaced the top of the tank, took another swig of coffee, and stepped out of the stall. I must have been more rattled than I thought, because I hadn't heard the door to the john open again. But it had, and there, blocking it, was a short, skinny man with red hair that looked like it had been brushed straight up all around his head, and a striped bow tie, red on black. He looked like a woodpecker accountant except for his smile. His smile bothered me. He was the guy I'd seen at Fred's funeral.

"You didn't flush," he said. He didn't move. "People ought to flush in public places."

"You're right—sorry," I said, and turned back to the stall. He was beside me before I saw him move, with his arm across my breast, grasping my right forearm—a perfect position to brace somebody, although his grip was carefully gentle.

"Ahh, that's okay," he smiled, and peered into the bowl. "Hey—you didn't even go!" He stopped smiling—it was like turning off a light switch—and his grip tightened. "What're you doing, hanging around public cans and not going. You ain't queer, are you?"

I thought I could probably take him. I've been decked often enough by short, wiry guys not to be fooled by their size. But I was armed—I had the coffee mug—and I always fight scared, which always makes me fight dirty. I needed to know more, though, if for nothing else, at least to get myself *good* and scared.

"O.K., rooster," I sighed, a lot more casually, I hoped, than I felt. "Let's have it. You either like to pick fights in bars or you think you've got business with me. You don't look drunk or beat-up enough for the first, so I'm betting on the second. Now, do you want to buy me another drink and we talk business, or do we have to play schoolyard games first?"

The smile clicked back on.

"*Rooster!*" he crowed. "The man says he doesn't want to hassle, and he calls me *rooster!* You fuckin' Irishman!"

I couldn't help myself. I started to smile back. "You prefer Woody?" I asked. "And by the way, I'm Czech."

The little man threw his head back and gave a pretty fair imitation of a real laugh. But as he did so he backed just out of my range. The little man new how to handle things, that was for sure.

"Jeezus," he chortled. "Woody! If I had a dollar for every time I heard that! All right, boopsie, you win. I just hadda be sure you didn't do something dumb, you dig?"

"I dig," I said. "Be prepared."

He laughed again and flashed me the boy scout sign. "That's me," he said, "still bucking for a merit badge. Oh, yeah, call me Knobby." He didn't offer to shake hands. "All right, what the hell, I'm supposed to deliver you pronto, but come on, I'll buy you a drink. I could use one myself. You do know enough not to try anything, don't you?"

I assured him I did. We strolled out of the john like old classmates. Knobby motioned me to my booth while he went to the bar—he was a cock-of-the-walk—and came back with another Irish coffee for me and a double Irish, hold the coffee, for himself.

"Cheers," I raised my mug. "Uh, Knobby, I don't suppose there's any chance you've got the wrong guy, is there?"

He threw back his head and laughed. It was enough to put you off laughing for a month.

"Hell, no, boopsie," he snickered. He reached into his side pocket and took out a newspaper clipping that he tossed at me. It was a picture of me, from a story about an insurance scam I had helped blow a few years ago . . . not a Karsh portrait, but like enough.

"Jeezus, man," Knobby went on, enjoying the hell out of himself, I thought, "I damn well *knew* you'd show up at the fucking funeral. Couldn't miss. So I just follow you from there to here, had me a few drinks while you went to the john, and then went in for the pickup. Garnish, I ain't got the wrong guy. Believe me."

A few drinks, had he said? Terrific. I figured it couldn't hurt to play weak and scared a little longer. Especially since I felt weak and scared. "O.K.," I said. "Are you supposed to toss me, or waste me, or what? I'd really like to know, man."

The laugh stopped and the smile clicked back on. "Hey, boopsie, *relax*," he said. "I don't know what you were doing in the can, or why I'm here, or whatever. I'm just a mailman, dig? I deliver you, I get a receipt, my tip, and ten-four, we *gone* and *down*. Nothing personal, you got it?" He finished his drink. "Come on, we gotta go."

"Just let me finish mine. Listen, you want another—on me?" I prefer fighting people drunker than I.

Don't tell, me, I already know: Paul Newman wouldn't play it that way. He would let himself be taken to wherever, just to gain another piece of the puzzle he was fitting together. And then when he'd found out everything his kidnapper had to tell him, he would wisecrack or punch his way out of the scene. But I had learned enough. To wit: I wasn't going to be hurt until we got to our destination; the people at our destination knew who I was, and knew a damned sight more about this whole business than I did; and, finally and most importantly, I didn't know that I wouldn't be hurt once we did get to wherever we were going. So

I'm not Newman. He gets paid more for playing at the job, anyhow, than I get for doing it.

I just hoped it would work, and it did. Knobby stared at his empty glass, at my half-full mug, and shrugged. "Well, O.K., Garnish, but then we gotta." Better and better. I was being as reasonable and docile as I knew how to be, and my new friend the rooster thought I was chicken. (And so I am; he just hadn't learned that that's what makes people most dangerous.) I took his glass back to the bar, rather than get a new one from the bartender. No point in diluting his John Locke with too much ice, now, was there?

No doubt about it, Knobby liked the stuff. He took a reverential sip as soon as I put the glass in his hand. I shoved my mug to one side of the table.

"Knobby, you're the politest kidnapper—sorry, mailman— I've met." He silently raised his glass, and sipped again. "But you didn't answer my first question. What mailbox are you supposed to deliver me to?"

"Huh?" Knobby grunted. It only took a second for him to get it, but it was an encouraging second; John Locke was dulling his wit and fogging his judgment. "Oh. Yeah. Well, boopsie, I guess I'm not supposed to tell you that. But you'll find out soon enough, anyhow. It ain't exactly a mailbox, you know? I mean, not a *male* box." He snickered. I love fighting people who snicker at their own jokes.

"You mean a woman?" I asked with my best I'm-dumb-but-I-think-I-get-it stare.

"Yah, but not just a woman, a lady. I'm delivering you for a personal interview with Mrs. Harmon Wright, my man. Don't know what she wants you for, but she does, and I'm taking you to her. Now," he swallowed the last of his whiskey, "let's go."

It was time. I rose, and as I rose I took my cigarettes out of my shirt pocket. I fished a book of matches out of my jacket.

Now there's a way of striking a match off an ordinary book, and setting the whole book afire in a sudden hiss of sulfur. Everybody who smokes has done it at least once, by accident. I had learned how to do it on purpose, and I did it now. As the book flared, I tossed it at Knobby's face. And as Knobby shouted and batted the flame away I kneed him once, carefully and not too gently, in the groin. But before he could double over in pain I had pulled his overcoat down, binding his shoulders, and spun him around in front of me, a writhing, gasping shield.

I'd assumed he would have a partner in the place; messengers like Knobby never travel alone. And, sure enough, a fellow twice my rooster's size was already halfway across the floor by the time I'd spun Knobby into position.

"Stop, asshole!" I barked at him. "Don't even think about it or I'll crack your friend's spine for him. You didn't sign on for an assault and battery charge, did you?" Of course I was the only guy in the bar who was liable for an assault and battery charge. But Knobby's backup didn't look all that much like the holder of a law degree. And besides, I had to say *something*.

It worked. He froze—my lucky day—at least long enough for me to shove the still-gasping Knobby at him and run like hell through the door. It couldn't have been more than five degrees Fahrenheit outside, and my overcoat was still lying in my booth. It didn't seem important.

There was the usual steady stream of traffic on Wacker, only moving slower and more erratically than usual because of the ice. I plunged into it, crossing Wacker to a chorus of honks and curses, dodging skidding cars like an all-American split end, and probably risking as much damage as if I had stayed with Knobby and King Kong. I made it, though and around the block and into an office building whose name I didn't notice, into the elevator and up to the seventh flor. (Whenever somebody says, "Pick a number," I always say "Seven.")

When I run away, I run away.

The seventh floor of the Mumble Building had some law offices, some nondescript and probably second-rate "consultants" in this and that, and finally, what I'd been looking for, a dentist. S. Kaminsky, D.D.S. I entered.

Nobody else was in the waiting room. The receptionist was reading *People* magazine, one of the office copies. It looked to be three or four weeks old. She seemed annoyed that I'd interrupted her studies.

"Yes, sir?" she said.

"Aah, I have an appointment for two o'clock. Mr. Garnish. It's my first visit here."

"Just a moment," she said, and checked her calendar. "I'm

sorry, Mr.—Garnish, but I don't seem to have you down for an appointment today."

"But you *must* have me down," I protested. "I specifically instructed my secretary to make it for today, at one. This is Dr. Kaminsky's office, isn't it?"

"Yes, it is. But," she checked her roster again, "I'm afraid you're just not here. And not tomorrow, either."

"But, ma'am, I am here. Oh, hell, I don't have time for this foolishness. Look—may I use your phone to call my office?"

"Well . . ." It was obviously counter to S. Kaminsky's standing orders, but I was a harassed businessman and she was a nice lady. I dialled the number Bridget had given me. Yolanda Wright's private number. Yolanda Wright's private number.

"Wright's residence," answered a woman's Spanish-inflected voice.

"Yes. Mrs. Wright, please. Harry Garnish here," I gruffed back, a boss asking for his screw-up secretary.

There was a ten-beat pause while I smiled, exasperated, at the receptionist (you just can't get a really efficeint secretary these days) and she smiled back (ah, yes, you *can*—just look at me!)

I heard the click of heels—probably on a parquet floor—approaching the phone at the other end.

"Hello. Hello, is this Mr. Garnish? I—"

"Oh, *hello*, Mrs. Wright," I boomed. "Listen, there's some sort of confusion about the appointment you set up for me. I'm afraid you must have gone about things the wrong way. Our friend Knobby," I winked at the receptionist, "seems rather fouled up about his delivery schedule also. Now, can you tell me where I'm supposed to be right now?"

She was quick enough. "Mr. Garnish, I'm *so* sorry if I've caused you any distress. That's why I have been trying to reach *you* all morning. I realized that there was no real need for Knobby to watch for you. Is he all right, by the way? You didn't —hurt him?"

From the tone of her voice she must have thought I was a karate black belt with the humanitarian instincts of a Waffen-SS man. Some lay people just think that way.

"That's neither here nor there, Mrs. Wright," I droned ominously. So *let* her think she was talking to Dirty Harry. "The point is, I'm a busy man, and I need to know where I am supposed to be right now. Perhaps we need a conference." I was sounding less and less like an irate boss, but the receptionist had dived back into *People* anyhow.

"Yes. Yes, I really do have to see you. But, will you trust me now? Mr. Garnish, this is very important to me. And believe me, I can make it all worth your while."

"That's fine, Yolanda. We obviously have to work this out from the beginning. Look. It's one now. Can you meet me in an hour in The Deli, in the Hancock Building?" The Deli was public enough for me to feel safe, and the Hancock was the home of Ecology International. I wanted to see just how afraid Mrs. Wright was of Mr. Wright in this thing, if at all—whatever this thing was.

There was the pause I had expected. "The Hancock. Couldn't you make it somewhere else?"

"Sorry, but I can't. I have an appointment there later this afternoon."

That was the hook. "All right. The Deli in one hour. I'll wait for you in the lobby. I'll be wearing a green suede coat." Swell. Whatever Mrs. Wright had to say to me, she wanted to say it before I saw her husband. But how had she known about Ryan's Pub? And, if she was the one who had gotten the key from the john, why did she have Knobby hang around waiting for *me*? And why me? Nobody was supposed to know about the business except Fred and me, and Fred was dead.

Had the bastard set me up, deliberately to put my butt in traction after they pulled his plug?

And, while we were giving ourselves headaches, what *was* in the box in Union Station, and why had it killed Fred—if it had?

Occam's razor, I thought, and laughed as I thanked the receptionist, mumbled something about mix-ups, and left the office: The simplest explanation is always the right one. Except when you're working with people, because they can't let themselves act simply, no matter how hard or how often they try it. Look at Fred and Marianne. Look at the Wrights. Look at me.

Occam should spend a month peeping in motels and tracing jumped checks.

And as I left the nameless building to walk back to my car I remembered that it was dead winter and that I didn't have my overcoat any more.

• 8

KNOBBY and Chewbacca would be long gone, I reasoned, especially since Ryan's bartender would have put in a beef to the Chicago P.D. But that also meant I couldn't waltz back in, reclaim my coat, and fandango out again unless I wanted to answer a lot of questions. I didn't.

So I did the next best thing. Trotted, freezing my pride off, to my car, drove ten blocks south to Marshall Field's, and another ten in a circle looking for a place to park; trotted, freezing my self-respect off, into Field's and bought a coat off the rack (thank God for charge cards) and took the bus up Michigan Avenue to the Hancock.

Before I left Field's, though, I decided that I ought, at least, to let my employer know where the hell I was. So I called the O'Toole Agency, where Brenda answered, and left a message that for the next hour or so I'd be lunching, on company business, of course, which also meant on company expense account, if I could swing it—at the Hancock Deli.

If Ryan's is one of my favorite bars, the Hancock is my favorite building, at least from the outside. It's a "skyscraper," I suppose, but a skyscraper so feisty it doesn't even have to be tall, planted like a pennant at the top of Lake Shore Drive, challenging the city and any architect in the place to come up with something to match its special arrogance. It's got all the vinegar and grace of a really good welterwight—and anybody will tell you that no heavyweight can hope to match that.

But only from the outside. Inside, it's as sterile and dull as any other place where a lot of big money is at pains to keep itself looking clean and smelling nice. And The Deli on the twelfth floor is about as much like a real deli as the jungle ride at Disneyland is like a trip up the Amazon.

Yolanda Wright needn't have worn her green suede coat, although it was a beautiful coat, and probably cost enough to keep a snow leopard in raw meat for a year. I would have recognized her anyway.

I had seen her pictures, I had watched her on television; I, like most of male Chicago, had wondered exactly what she was like, and if she could possibly be as good, as exciting, as she looked. With or without the green coat, she was a slim, tall blonde, with eyes that flashed intelligence and a mouth that signalled sensuality, and a body—how many bodies like that have *you* seen?—absolutely in control of her will. "Sexy" is a word you use for the girls you see on the cover of drugstore magazines, and "classy" is a word you use for women you think you'll never be able to touch, though you'd like to. The two ideas ought to be mutually exclusive, and it was part of the fascination of Yolanda Wright that she seemed so perfectly to fulfill both of them.

I recognized her at once, as I said. I'd thought about her a lot.

What interested me, though, was how she knew that *I* was there so quickly. I had expected her to be flustered, nervous—you know, the way beautiful blondes always act when they meet hard-boiled private eyes. Instead, she flicked a glance at me as I walked into the lobby, nodded sharply—the way you nod when you say, "Heel, Spot!" and Spot trots up—and paced across the carpet toward me like she owned the place. Of course, to all intents and purposes, she did.

"Mr. Garnish," she smiled as she held out her hand. "I have to apologize for any trouble I've caused you. Please believe me, I didn't mean to." It didn't sound like an apology.

"Right, Mrs. Wright," I said smiling back. "Attempted kidnapping is a little out of my ordinary line. But I'm sure you have some reason for it, since people usually do."

Her smile froze. I had been rude. I sure the hell had tried to be rude.

"Yes," she said, with that arctic smile. "I did have a reason, as you so charitably suppose. But will you join me for lunch? I'm quite sure we can talk this all out, to our mutual satisfaction."

I never pass up a free lunch, so I agreed. At two o'clock in the afternoon, the place was almost empty. I looked around quickly, apprehensively, for my old pal Knobby—after all, I didn't know how much I could trust Mrs. Wright—but he was nowhere in sight. Just a few fellows in sleek three-piece suits, polishing off their chef's salads before they trudged back to the office to write slogans for soap.

Our waiter arrived almost as soon as we sat down. At two in the afternoon, you want to clear people the hell out and get ready for the dinner rush.

"Mr. Garnish—may I call you Harry?" I stared and said nothing. "Would you care for some wine?"

"No, thanks, Yolanda," I said. "And, by the way, it's my treat." Turning to the waiter, I ordered a Reuben sandwich and a bottle of Heineken's, and a glass of Chablis for the lady. The lady smiled uncertainly and ordered a shrimp salad to go with her wine.

When the drinks came, I took a grateful gulp of the beer and decided that it was about time to behave seriously. "Mrs. Wright," I said. "You called my office this morning. You've had a man waiting for me at Ryan's Pub for three days. You obviously want something from me in a pretty bad way. All I want to know is what, and why, if it isn't too much trouble?"

She took a tiny sip of wine, put the glass down, and then took another. "Mr. Garnish—Harry—I know that you know who my husband is, and what he stands for."

I don't know what anybody stands for, present company included, but I nodded like I did.

"Well, she went on, "then you must also know that Harmon and his cause"—she said "His Cause" with capital letters—"are very vulnerable to any hints or threats of scandal. And scandal is what we're talking about, Harry. That's all I can tell you, except that, for God's sake, I *have* to have that package. Not just for me or for Harmon, but for everything Harmon stands for, you must give it to me. And, as I said, I can make it well worth the trouble to you."

I stared. I've found it generally the best thing to do when you don't know what the hell is going on. Then she didn't have the package. So who did? So who knew? So who could find out? Lunch arrived.

I hadn't eaten since before playing Fred's tape, and I was hungry. And the Reuben sandwich, one of the great inventions of

51 •

Western civilization, is a meal that *nobody* can make badly. Except in Indiana.

"Listen, I'd really like to help you," I vocalized through corned beef and sauerkraut. "Believe me, I would. But, honest, Mrs. Wright, I don't have a package for you or anybody else, and I don't even know what this whole scenario is about. I walked into Ryan's Pub, I got hassled by a twerp who said he was working for you, and now this."

It must've sounded convincing, because she put her fork down without taking her first bit of shrimp.

"You mean you *don't* have the package? But Mr. Healey said . . ."

"Mr. Healey said what?" And now I put my sandwich down. "What does he have to do with you and your husband, and how the hell do you get from him to me? You know he's dead, by the way, don't you? They planted him this morning. Of course, you don't have to tell me a goddamned thing." I was getting flustered, more, maybe, than I'd meant to get. "But believe me, lady, if you don't, there's a strong chance you'll wind up telling it to the cops. And they'll make you buy your *own* lunch!"

It was a dumb enough thing to say that we both stared, after I had said it, and burst out laughing, though neither of us wanted to. Anyhow, it relaxed her—a little.

"All right," she said, shaking her head. She had a pretty head. "I'll be perfectly honest with you, Mr. Garnish. But let's both play that game. You have to admit that you weren't in Ryan's Pub by accident today, and you also have to admit that there *is* a package."

"Call me Harry," I said again. "About Ryan's, you've got me dead to rights. And as for the package, I'll admit at least that I believe there's such a thing somewhere. So?"

"So, Harry. The package that you believe exists, and that I know exists, contains two pounds of pure cocaine. Does that surprise you?"

"Not particularly," I said, finishing my Heineken's. "Packages can contain lots of things: money, jewels, even body parts. But packages with drugs in them are the kind people tend to get most excited about. And, excuse me for saying this, Mrs. W., but coke is the drug I'd most associate with folks from your set. The expensive set, I mean."

She was not amused. "Oh, Jesus," she sighed, "you're one of *those*. One of those shrivelled little people who like to believe the worst about people with real money, just because we do have real money. You're just too happy, aren't you," she glared at me, "to believe the worst you can cook up in that tacky little brain of yours?

"Yes, all right, it *was* cocaine! And yes, all right, cocaine *is* an expensive drug, and it does have a certain currency among some people I know. So what do you care when I tell you I've never used it, and neither has my husband, nor ever bought it for our friends? You won't believe me, will you? Because you're so damned sure that my type all use it, and you're so damned eager to believe that my type doesn't have worry in the world except how to get it." She finished her wine and all but slammed the glass on the table. "Why the hell should I even try to talk to you? Just forget I approached you—O.K.?"

But before she could rise I laid my hand on her arm. "No. Wait," I said. "Look, I don't have many talents, but knowing when I've said the wrong thing is one of them. Go on. Please."

She did, with a little smile. "Sorry. Even if you don't feel that way, you know what I'm talking about." I knew. In fact, I did feel that way.

"But, you see," she continued, "it's not the cocaine that matters. It's the connection with Harmon, and with Ecology International. The amount in question could be worth several million dollars, and *we* could be suspected of . . . of . . . *pushing* it. It's the sort of thing that could satisfy everybody's worst suspicions about the idle, corrupt rich, and set E.I. and the cause back for years."

"No, I don't see," I said. "What does a pack of coke have to do with you, your husband, and the cause?" By golly, *I* was beginning to say it with a capital "C."

"The *wrapper*, of course!" She sounded exasperated at my stupidity. "The cocaine is in an E.I. shipping wrapper. Look." She put down her fork and leaned toward me. "Your friend Mr. Healey was doing some employee surveillance for us. Just the normal checks on people we might like to promote, or hire, background, credit ratings, things like that." Things like that, I reflected, were once one's own damn business, but that was when I and the world were young.

"So," my wealthy lunch guest went on, "about a month ago, Mr. Healey came to me—to *me*, mind you—and told me he thought one of our people was involved in something illegal, something dangerous."

"Smuggling coke?" I asked, stifling a yawn.

"Yes! Yes, you see, we have a number of projects in South America. A number of species there . . ."

"Are endangered," I finished for her. "And that means you have a lot of mail coming from and going to Colombia, Argentina, wherever, and with a classy letterhead and clout like yours, it's a perfect channel for grade-A nose candy. And while two pounds of coke wouldn't put a dent in your mad money for the month, the street price of the stuff could support a starving village in India for a couple of years at least. Uh, look. Somebody in your organization wouldn't have Fred killed because he tumbled onto this scam, would they?"

It took her a couple of beats before she realized what I had asked her. Her shock sounded sincere.

"Good God, you can't really mean that! Are you crazy? I wanted to see you because I thought you might help find out who *did* kill Fred—Mr. Healey."

"But *you* might know he'd found a two-pound package of coke, and *you* might know where he stashed it and *you* knew who would come looking for it. That interests me, you know?" A lot of things interested me at the moment, but foremost among them was whether somebody besides me and Fred knew about the damned *key*. Or was the package of coke—whatever it meant, finally, in this whole mess—still nestled safely in a numbered storage box in Union Station?

"No, no, you've got it all wrong," said Yolanda Wright, a lot calmer than I would have been in her place. "I had Knobby waiting for you because Fred, Mr. Healey, always spoke of you as one of his best friends, and because he told me, if anything happened to him, I should contact you. He didn't say why, but he obviously thought it was important."

That didn't wash at all, but I let it pass for the moment. What interested me more was the fact that twice, now, she had referred to my dead friend by his first name, and corrected herself to call him "Mr. Healey."

"Go on," I grunted, lighting a cigarette.

"Well," her nibs said, "Mr. Healey, checking into some recent E.I. transactions, discovered this package of—of *coke*." She laughed as she said it, as if she'd never used the word before to refer to anything but a soft drink. "Mr. Garnish, I swear that the first time I knew about the package *or* about Mr. Healey was when he called it to my attention, and asked for my help."

"Your help?" I asked. A paid private investigator rarely asks amateurs for assistance. It can cut into accounts payable.

"Yes, my help," she replied. "He was worried, you see, that what he'd found might be too big or too dangerous or too, well, just too complicated for the job he'd been hired to do. So naturally he came to me, since he didn't want to cause a scandal but also didn't want to ignore possibly harmful information."

"Naturally. And you told him to wait and see what developed, right?"

She looked surprised. "How did you know?"

"Because it's what people usually say when they're in trouble but don't know how much. All right, to whom was the package addressed?"

"I don't know. I never saw it. Mr. Healey was in the office the day it arrived, and he said he'd taken it with him for safekeeping, and for evidence, if we should want to do anything about it."

"And how much did he want?"

"I beg your pardon?"

"How much did Fred want to keep it all quiet?"

"Harry. This was *not* blackmail. Mr. Healey knew that it would upset Harmon if he knew his project was being used to smuggle dope into the country, and he took the package to *protect* him—to protect everyone. He never even asked for an extra cent for hiding it. It's how I knew he was being honest with me—with us."

I didn't say anything, although it all fitted in with the Fred I had known, not the one I'd heard on the tape. Not a hero, not a tough guy—in fact, a bit of a put-upon, passive guy. But honorable. Somehow, even over drinks and sandwiches in the Hancock, it mattered.

"I'm glad," I said. "Now, did your husband ever learn about the coke? And, speaking of the coke, where is it? And how the hell did I get mixed up in all this? Fred may have told you to contact me, but did he tell you to look for me in Ryan's?"

"Harmon still doesn't know, of course. It would hurt him terribly to find out that his work was being used for—for this. You don't know how much he believes, how much he's invested in this cause. No," she said, catching my smile, "I don't mean just money, Mr. Garnish, I mean how much he's invested of *himself*. But perhaps you don't believe a man can actually be committed to something larger than his own self-interest."

"Oh, I've heard rumors that it happens in some circles," I said, flipping my credit card to the waiter. "But you've only answered one question."

"Yes, I know. Mr. Healey never told me where the package was; he said it would be better for me not to know. But he called me Wednesday night—Harmon was out—and I think he was, well, intoxicated, because he was rambling, confused, and he sounded terribly worried about something. What, precisely, he wouldn't say. But he did keep mentioning Ryan's Pub, and some kind of 'insurance policy'. Do you know what that could have meant?"

"Beats me," I lied. "Go on."

"Well, when I heard he'd died, Friday morning, I was sure it had something to do with our—our problem. But I didn't know what to *do*! I couldn't go to Harmon, and I *couldn't* go to the police. Can you imagine what they, and the newspapers, would have done to Ecology International with a story like this?"

I could imagine. Poor, rich, dedicated Harmon Wright would be lucky to come out of it wearing nothing worse than a Murray the Clown suit.

"So I called Knobby. Knobby's done—things for us in the past, and it was all I could think of to do. I asked him to, I suppose you would say 'case' Ryan's Pub, stay around the place for a few days if he couldn't find anything, and let me, *only* me, know if anything developed. As an afterthought, really, I asked him to obtain a photograph or a description of you, in case you went to Ryan's. You were a very difficult man to get in touch with this weekend, you know. But, please believe me, I never meant for it to come to violence or coercion."

"Few people do mean things to come out that way," I grunted.

"It just turns out that way, a lot of the time. But you really mean this whole mess is just to get back a package you've never even seen, and to spare your hubby a little worry?"

She flared. "He is *not* my 'hubby,' he is my *husband,* and I love him very much. And it is *not* a 'little worry,' as I've been trying to explain to you. It's his *life.*"

She really meant it. While I felt cheap and took the latest reading on my goon barometer, she sipped some wine and calmed down.

"I'm sorry," she said. "I realize that, not knowing Harmon, you couldn't understand what he's really like. But I wanted to see you to ask for your help, Mr. Garnish. If you and your agency could possibly finish what Mr. Healey started, if you could give me any help at all, I would be very grateful."

I got up. "Sorry," I said. "In the first place, I don't know if you've really told me everything you know. In the second place, *whatever* you know is now evidence in a homicide investigation, and I'm afraid you're going to have to take it to the cops sooner or later, dirty linen and all—sooner being better for everybody concerned. If Fred didn't tell you that from the beginning, he was getting stupid in his old age. And in the third place—"

"In the third place it isn't his agency, Mrs. Wright. It's mine. I wonder if you would be kind enough to explain a few more details to *me*? Hello, Harry."

I hate it when people creep up behind me and speak just over my shoulder. Especially when it's Bridget O'Toole who does it.

• 9

FOR it was she. In all her pudgy glory, in a flowing polyester construction that looked like a banner for the Orange Bowl pageant or like sunset over the steel works—there she stood.

Not that Mrs. Garnish raised any rude children. "Mrs. Wright," I said, "Miss O'Toole, my employer. Bridget," I said with what I devoutly hoped was an icy stare, "Mrs. Wright. Won't you sit down?"

I was angry that she'd followed me, though of course I could imagine why she had. I was staying away from work, so naturally she was convinced it meant something important. You'd be surprised how conscientious people are about their work calendars. I once knew a rapist who—honest—only raped during his lunch hour. The guy would be normal as pasteurized process cheese until twelve noon. Then he would leave work, do a number of horrible things, and be back smiling and straight-arrow by one-thirty (he worked for city hall so nobody even noticed the hour-and-a-half lunch hour). If we're creatures at all, we're creatures of Habit.

If I was annoyed, though, my lunch partner was livid. Oh, I know you've heard the word before—livid with anger, livid with rage, and so forth. But do you know what the word really means? No, not red; it means "white." *Pale* will do, although it doesn't quite describe the lividness—lividity?—of Yolanda Wright when she discovered somebody else had heard most of our conversation.

"Don't worry, Mrs. Wright—may I call you Yolanda?" Bridget said as she sank into the empty chair at our table. "I have no intention of violating any confidences you may have shared with Mr. Garnish here, and I certainly have no intention of making your life more complicated than it already sounds. Oh yes, I would like a cup of coffee." The waiter had just returned to our table, puzzled that his customers had multiplied.

Bridget went on. "I'm really very sorry if this seems forward of me, but I *do* know about your little problem, Mrs. Wright, with Ryan's Pub and Mr. Garnish here, and I also know that you must be very concerned about the fate of the package you are trying so hard to locate."

I promised myself, silently, that I would kill this woman at the first opportunity.

"And do you mind telling me how you know all this, Miss— O'Toole, is it?" It was the tone of voice she reserved, I guessed, for dressmakers and downstairs maids, if her type still had downstairs maids. All I knew was what I saw on public television.

Bridget, benevolent, beamed. And then, looking at me, blushed. I was, after all, "Father's brightest young man," and the chief operative of this high class outfit; or so it said in the fine print.

"Well," she mumbled as her coffee came. "Finding you was really not difficult, and I fear I did hear a bit of your conversation with Harry here before I announced myself. But, seriously, dear," and now for the first time she turned her sympathetic gaze full on Yolanda Wright, "don't you think we ought to be talking about your problem, and not just the accident of my presence?"

That "dear" of Bridget's works wonders; it's so smarmy and so confiding. Now, now, dear, you just tell Sister Mary Godzilla what's bothering you, and she'll try to put everything right. And she uses it like a precision tool. I wondered how many sixth grade kids she'd wheedled into turning informer on who, exactly, poured the chocolate milk down Debbie's back at recess.

Anyhow, it was working today. Mrs. Wright opened up and spilled everything she'd just told me in the strictest, most solemn confidence. Bridget nodded and grunted sympathetically throughout the story, as if she really did understand what was going on. I sure as hell didn't, and so I sat and played with my spoon and lit two cigarettes.

"Very good, Yolanda," said Bridget at the end of the tale. She could have been approving a description of the Alps by a geography student. "Yes, very good, indeed. But do you mind, dear, if I ask you just a few more questions? Just so that I can get things clear in my own head, you see."

Given the tone of voice Bridget asked in, lovely Yolanda had the option of saying, "Yes," or leaping in guilt and shame out of the nearest window. She said, "Yes. Go on."

"Fine, then. Now. There are three men standing just outside the lobby of this restaurant who are obviously supposed to be here to do something to, or about, Mr. Garnish as he leaves. Could you, please, ask them to leave?"

I sneaked a glance over my shoulder at the entrance, hoping to salvage my pride. I didn't. There they were, big as life, Knobby among them. I looked back at Yolanda Wright, who, smiling, nodded and sent a hand signal to them. They melted away.

"They were only for my protection," she said to Bridget. "Mr. Garnish was never in any danger."

"Well, thank you, dear. I'm glad to hear you weren't planning anything unpleasant, but I do have to look out for my own, you know." *Her* own? I thought. On a cold day in hell! But I had lost the ball by that time, anyway.

"And now," Bridget went on. "Do you really understand that, as you sit here, you are in the process of committing a felony? In fact, a number of felonies. You are admitting that you have concealed evidence in the murder of Fred Healey, you are admitting to instigating a plot to kidnap my friend and assistant Harry, and you are admitting to collusion in the importation of illegal drugs. And also, dear, by signalling to those three men to leave the lobby, you are admitting, before witnesses, to what amounts to an assault charge."

I would have stopped her, but she was enjoying it too much.

Mrs. Wright wasn't. The friendly, dough-faced, bumbling little old lady was coming on like an assistant D.A. up for reelection, and Yolanda was both shocked and scared. She began to rise from her chair when my boss stopped her—and stopped her with a whisper that was like a slap on the wrist.

"Sit *down*, Missy!" she snapped. Yolanda Wright sat down. "Now, I don't care *how* much money you have, or *how* many people you have working for you, or *how* many people you think you can buy. Right now, young lady, your fat is in the *fire*. You put it there, and I might be able to pull it out. Or would you rather sit and watch it roast?"

I had never seen her like this, in two years of working with— O.K., O.K., *for*—her. But whether she was acting or really believed what she said, she was damned impressive. And I wasn't the only one who thought so.

"What do you want to know?" said Yolanda Wright.

Bridget sighed and relaxed. It was like watching a circus tent fall in on itself.

"Oh, nothing very difficult. Just, for instance, *who* was the packet of cocaine addressed to at Ecology International?"

"Uh—it was addressed to Clyde Crews." Dammit, *I* had asked her that and she'd answered with a lie.

"But he's just the coordinator who handles all our mail from Central and South America. I'm sure that he would never get involved in something like this."

"Well, perhaps not," said Bridget. "And now, dear, another question. Had you been having an—an—affair with Fred Healey? And for how long?"

No, no, Yolanda didn't jump, or drop her coffee cup, or swallow her spoon. She didn't even flinch. That's how I knew she had been waiting for that question since we first sat down.

But hell, Fred and Yolanda Wright? It didn't make sense.

"Only about five or six months," said Yolanda. "Until—until now." She looked at Bridget with the kind of stare you reserve for the fortune teller who's just described the pentagon birthmark on your ass.

Bridget seemed unfazed. "That's a fine answer, dear. And now, just to retain you as our client, I'll take a hundred dollars from you. A check will be perfectly acceptable, and we have your phone number, of course. Thank you for being so helpful. Harry, have you finished yet?"

I had, in more ways than one, I thought to myself. Without any more talk, Mrs. Wright fished in her purse, handed some bills over to Bridget, and we all rose. It was late in the afternoon, the beer was starting to get to me, my head hurt, and I knew I had no reason to be angry at Bridget but I was. As she and I walked out of The Deli I let her know; Mrs. Garnish didn't raise any shy children, either.

"Bridget, what the *hell* do you think you're doing here?" I hissed on our way to the elevator. "Goddamn it, I've been braced, punched, and generally fucked over all day, and now you show up and behave like it's all a high school quiz. Do you know I was trying to do something for *Fred—poor* Fred—when I started out this morning? Do you know what you've just let the agency in for? Damn! Do you know that, back in my apartment . . ."

"Shut up, Harry!" she snapped, just the way she had snapped at Mrs. Wright back in The Deli. I shut up. "I don't want to hear a thing about what you may have back at your apartment. I don't want to hear a thing about anything you know about poor Fred's death that isn't already public knowledge. Because if you tell me, I am mortally bound to tell the police, and to tell them who I heard it from. Poor Mrs. Wright is a client—much good may it do her—you saw her pay me—so I don't have to, in fact I can't, reveal any of her secrets. But you, Harry, you're my partner. Now—" by then we were walking out the front door of the Hancock, into the Chicago deepfreeze—"where do we go now?"

There's an old Czech curse that, loosely translated, means, "May you find yourself in midlife in the employ of someone you don't respect who is smarter than you."

All right, there isn't an old Czech curse like that. But there ought to be. If I ever learn my father's native language, I'll make it up myself.

Where did we go now? "Bridget," I said, shouting over the traffic and the wind of Michigan Avenue, "I really ought to see Harmon Wright. He's on the tenth floor of the Hancock. Why don't you take the CTA back home?"

It was almost four o'clock. And by four, in Chicago, in winter, night has already fallen. The sun has checked out for the day anyhow and left the sky the color of a very large, used litter box. Downtown, it smells like that, too.

But Bridget didn't want to leave.

"I believe we *should* see Mr. Wright," she said. "But, since Mrs. Wright is now our client, I can't think of a pretext for barging into his office with all the facts we have—can you?"

She may have really been asking for advice or she may have been trying to compensate for the mess I had made of things. Either way, it was a nice thing to say.

"Well," I improvised, "suppose O'Toole Agency was interested in making a big contribution to the work of Ecology International, and just wanted the bossman to reassure us about what splendid guys they really are. Think that could get us in?"

"Oh, *good,* Harry! But maybe we needn't identify ourselves as a detective agency. Don't you think Mr. Wright, despite what his wife says, might be expecting to hear from people of, well, of our sort?"

Of course he would. Fred had told me so much on the tape, and I had forgotten. We decided that Wright might even be waiting for somebody meeting my description. So, we agreed, Bridget would go alone—a wealthy, dotty older lady with a yen for endangered animals—to see what she could see while I hung around the Hancock lobby.

It had been a hell of a day. I'd heard from a dead friend, damn near been kidnapped, lost my overcoat, met my first sexy millionaire, and now I was sending my flaky boss to do a job that should have been mine.

As we waited for one of the elevators to hit the ground floor, I asked one last question.

"Bridget?"

"Yes, Harry?"

"How did you know Yolanda Wright was sleeping with Fred Healey?"

The elevator doors were closing as she smiled at me, shaking her head. "Oh, Harry, surely you don't believe *everything* people tell you!"

Huh?

• 10

Bridget was in the office of Harmon Wright for at least an hour. Don't ask me how she bluffed her way in, or what they talked about for that long. She has her ways. And when she met me back down in the lobby, she only grimaced at me, and said, "That is not a nice man."

"Very helpful information, Bridget," I grumbled. "Did you find out anything about the missing coke, or about Fred's connection with Ecology International?"

"Well, no, dear, not really. I did find out, though, that Mr. Wright is a very vain man—an unbalanced man, I should say. He *is,* I believe, passionately committed to the idea of saving endangered species of animals. He talks about it with real emotion, but—do you know?—with an emotion that almost frightens one, as if—I don't know—as if he was almost more concerned with blaming people for the disappearance of the animals than with saving them. Oh," she smiled at me, "I know none of this makes much sense. Maybe we should all just try to sleep on things."

That sounded great to me, except I wanted to know just what it was I was supposed to sleep on. "Fine," I said. "So you think Harmon Wright, one of the most prominent people in Chicago, is a nut. Do you think he's enough of a nut to have killed Fred, just for the sake of preserving the pure name of Ecology International? And does *he* suspect his wife of sleeping with Fred?"

I'd noticed, ever since I'd begun asking Bridget questions, that I was asking questions designed to let Yolanda Wright, that slim and troubled lady, off the hook. I hoped Bridget didn't notice this, too. If she did, she didn't inflict it on me.

"Oh, Harry, it's late," she sighed. "And I'm very tired."

Yeah. Well. "And Yolanda Wright?" I asked.

"Oh, Yolanda Wright. Well, Harry dear, I'd be very careful if you meet that young woman again. And I'm sure," she looked at me, "you will."

She hadn't mentioned it, but I knew she needed a ride home; she was walking with me to my car. It's that nun training, you know; they get used to being *driven* places.

We sailed up Lake Shore Drive in silence. Or, rather, with those mumbled empty comments—("Don't you think they could salt the Drive better in winter?" "Oh, the city hasn't been the same since Daley died.")—that area less acceptable substitute for silence.

I sailed to the front of Bridget's house (it used to be Martin O'Toole's house, a big drafty mansion in Wilmette) the way you sail a two-man skiff: tacking on the ice so as to cut back to starboard just as the car stopped floating and just before it hit the curb. Chicago life in wintertime is a matter of such small but essential skills. Bridget maneuvered onto the sidewalk, thanked me for the ride, and waddle-skated to her door. After I was sure she was securely home and the porch light turned off, I began sailing back to my own place, five miles due south.

I hoped to sleep late the next day, Tuesday. Of course I always hope to sleep late, but this time I thought I had really earned it. So it was with less than a choirboy smile that I answered my phone when it rang at eight in the morning.

"Garnish? Carp, Skokie P.D."

Imagine that the collection agency comes to repossess your stereo while you're just pouring cocktails for yourself and Audrey Hepburn. That's how it feels to get a message from Inspector Carp.

"Oh. Hello, Clarence. What can I do for you?" Clarence Carp hates to be called Clarence, particularly by the scum of the earth.

"You know damned well what you can do for me, Garnish. And you better do it for yourself, too. You can haul your two-bit ass down here, this morning, before I have to send somebody after you. And we wouldn't like that, would we?"

"Ah, no, Clarence, I don't guess we would. Would nine o'clock or so be O.K.?"

Inspector Carp thought nine o'clock would be lovely.

I've never seen a real carp. I mean, not face-to-face—just fried and breaded on plates, with saffron rice. But I have always thought that Clarence Carp, if he could meet his fishy namesakes, would have a lot to talk about with them.

He isn't really scaly, mind you, though his face is a kind of living memorial to some epic, teenage battle with acne. But no, it's his eyes that give him what I think of as the real carp look: an anxious predator, pretty low down on the food chain.

He must blink. We all do. But I swear I have never caught him at it.

"Garnish, why the hell didn't you check in yesterday after I left a message for you?" He said this as a cop closed the door to his office. I took a seat, without being asked, and got a cigarette lit before I answered.

"I notice there's no stenographer here, Inspector. Is this an official interview or not? Because if it isn't, I'm leaving right now."

Carp smiled. "Harry, Harry, you sad little clown. You know goddamn well what this is, and you know you're not walking out of here before we've had our little chat. You want to call a lawyer? Really—do you, Harry?"

Part of being a really successful rat, which means a really surviving one, is knowing when not to push. I shook my head at Carp and settled back in my chair.

"Swell," he sighed. "Peachy. Now. Who do you think took a shot at Marianne Healey, and why?"

"Inspector, I wish the hell I knew. She came to see me about poor Fred's death—you know, friend of the family, like that. We talked for a while about how awful it all was, I told her to count on me for the funeral arrangements, and while I was walking her to her car—bang! Honest, that's all I know."

Carp smiled even wider, shook his head, and picked up his phone, punching an interoffice line. "Sally, no calls for a while, please," he said in a gentle voice.

"Now, schmuck, you know you gotta do better than that, at least if you want to walk out of here today. You weren't a friend of the family, Harry. You were fucking the brains out of your old buddy's old lady, and everybody—*everybody*, man—knew it. You amaze me, you know that? You spend your life chasing down other guys cheating, and then when you start a little horizontal hopping on the side, you think you're all of a sudden the Invisible Man. Jesus."

Inspector Carp, if I forgot to mention it, is not a charming man.

"So, anyhow," he went on. "I figure you could be a prime candidate for snuffing Healey. Except you probably wouldn't have the balls for it, and except you probably didn't care about the twist anyhow. But I planned to run you in Friday, just for the fun of it. Caceres from Evanston was keeping an eye on you while I got the paperwork done, you know? And then the bitch gets shot practically in your arms, so I figure, hell, let's wait and see if old Garnish there leads us anywhere interesting.

"And you did, Harry, you did. So what was all that crap yesterday with you and Goofy O'Toole and Yolanda Wright, up at the Hancock? You ain't thinking about trying to bang the Wright woman next, are you? Or, maybe your bull dyke boss is?"

I was at the door before he could hit the intercom. "Sally, whoever the hell Sally is, get your butt in here on the *double!*" I roared into the outer office. I probably should have been an army officer, because it worked—the Voice of Command, I mean. A secretary who looked like Olive Oyl, outfitted by Frederick's of Hollywood, got her butt—what there was of it—in there on the double. I left the door open. A couple of uniforms were heading for the office, looking unhappy with me, and I wanted them to hear this, too.

"O.K., Sally, thank you. I need a witness for this, because there may be legal charges against your boss." I was still shouting, drowning out Carp's enraged gurgles. "Inspector Carp has been conducting an unwitnessed, illegal interrogation on unspecified charges, and in the course of it he has bullied me, insulted a Mrs. Marianne Healey, a widow now recovering from gunshot wounds, and has just slandered my employer, Miss Bridget O'Toole, implying that she is a lesbian. Anything further said between us I want you to hear, and you guys, too, if you're not busy," I said to the cops who were just outside the door. They tried hard not to grin. One of them, Wally Rosenblatt, was an old poker buddy of mine, like Al Caceres. Clarence Carp, who I knew from a lot of late night comments over beer and pretzels, was not well-loved by his subordinates.

I should have been enjoying it all, too. But, dammit, I really was mad. Don't ask me why. It was a dumb way to react and Carp, the bastard, had been trying to bait me. But knowing things and acting intelligently on what I know has always been a trick I haven't quite got the hang of.

"Now, Inspector Carp," I continued. I hadn't paused for breath, although I noticed I had lit another cigarette—with shaking hands. "You just asked me if Miss Bridget O'Toole and Mrs. Yolanda Wright were having, or contemplating, a homosexual affair. My answer, Inspector, is no, not to the best of my knowledge. And I can also tell you that Miss O'Toole is representing Mrs. Wright in some matters which I *will not* disclose to you unless you want to get a court order. Is there anything else you would like to ask me—before witnesses, that is?"

"Garnish, you know damned well I never suggested any such things." Carp was as red as I'd ever seen him. "But this interview is over. And if you *do* get any ideas about slander charges, you better realize that you're the one who's slandered *me* of what you can't prove. And before witnesses."

It's what I always do when I get righteous. Make an ass of myself, that is. It's why I try never to get righteous.

"Now," continued Carp, "you can go. But, my friend, you'll be hearing from me again on this thing. Thanks for your cooperation."

Carp turned back to the papers on his desk, the cops shrugged at one another, Olive Oyl looked like she didn't know where the hell she was supposed to be. I grumped my way back to my car, feeling everybody's eyes on my damnfool back as I left. Well, at least they'd all have something to talk about on their coffee break—the noisy idiot who had gone up against Carp. And lost. Because I had.

Sure, Carp was mad as hell. But that's when he's happiest, and my grandstand act had given him exactly what he'd wanted, with the bonus, for him, of ruining my day. He didn't really give a rat's ass, it dawned on me, who had killed Fred, or even who had shot Marianne.

What he was interested in was the Wright connection. And why? I wondered. The Wrights were *very* big in Chicago. Had somebody from city hall sent word to the boondock P.D.'s about them? And if so, what word? They were as pure, as far as anybody knew, as a bottle of factory-fresh aspirin. So were they being protected, or was somebody trying to unprotect them? And what did the Wrights *really* have to do with Fred's death?

I mean, a very unimportant private eye comes into possession of evidence that can bring down a very important, very millionaire ecologist. Yes? No, friends—only in books, not in Chicago. Not even if he *has* been screwing the millionaire's lady. And, after all, what evidence did we have for that? Just Bridget's rabbit-out-of-the-hat leap of insight, that Bridget herself had later disowned. If things were as screwy as they looked to be in this whole affair, mightn't Yolanda Wright want us to think we were as smart as we acted, just to protect her interest—whatever *that* was?

And yet, back in my apartment was a tape cassette nobody else had heard, by a dead man who knew he was about to die. And it said, if it said nothing else, that the whole silly business was real, even if it didn't make any sense. Unless, of course, Fred was trying to pull one last flummox on me, "from beyond the grave," as the magazines all said.

The hell with it. I wished I were home in bed. And I wished it even more when I pulled out of the Skokie Police Department lot, checked my rear view mirror, and saw there—surprise, surprise—the face of my old drinking buddy, Knobby. Knobby had a gun. Don't ask me what kind of gun, they all look the same to me—ugly.

"Hello, Harry! Just keep driving toward the lake," Knobby said, and chortled.

Click.

· 11

"WHADDYA say, Harry—buy me another drink?" The little rooster man laughed at his own joke. I didn't think I was required to join in.

"Uh, Knobby," I said. "Do you mind if I ask? Is this a personal call, or are you on business?"

"Oh, it's business all right, boopsie. Course, you and I still have some personal things to settle, right? But I figure there's plenty of time for that—you know, like some night when you got nothing to do and don't expect no visitors. But today, I am on the payroll. Just head for Sheridan and turn north." I suppose my icy calm expression—never one of my best—was more off than usual that day. Because, catching sight of my face in the rearview mirror, Knobby clicked his smile back into full gear and said, "Hey, really, boopsie, relax. Nothing very bad is going to happen to you—today, anyhow."

"Knobby, what a tower of strength you are to me," I grimaced. And he threw his head back and crowed. It's stupid, I know, but I was almost beginning to like the little sonofabitch.

"Well, while I've got you in a good mood," I continued, "would you mind telling me whose payroll we're on today? Is it Mrs. Wright again?"

"'Samatter, Harry, don't you like surprises? You sure the hell like to *give* 'em," he said, rubbing his jaw. (He should have been rubbing his balls, as I remembered our last encounter, but I suppose even kidnappers have their etiquette.)

"No," he went on. "It ain't Mrs. Wright today, I'll tell you that much. And as for the rest, you just gotta wait." And he settled back in his seat, cradling his gun in his lap, looking like a guy who had just put a third house on Boardwalk with a hotel already on Park Place: a self-satisfied prick, in other words.

We hit Sheridan Road and turned north, left, if you don't know Chicago, where the lake is always east and so where the natives always give directions by compass points, much to the dismay of out-of-towners.

The weather hadn't exactly gotten better since Friday, but it had gotten miserable in a different way, which is what you come to expect in my hometown. Instead of clear bright skies and hell-froze-over temperatures, today's treat from the winter god of Chicago (a psychopathic ex-wrestler, I was convinced) was thirty-three degrees, no sun, and light wet snow. It felt like driving over a field of underdone dumplings.

At least the dumplings, like a squishy Yellow Brick Road, were leading me toward Chicago's own kingdom of Oz. Starting from South Evanston, the further north you go along Sheridan Road, coasting the lake, the richer the real estate gets and the more invisible to the mortal eye the real estate owners become. Wilmette, Winnetka, and finally Kenilworth. They've all got to have their poor folks, I suppose. It's just that the poor folks from those townships could come on like Good King Wenceslaus to the *middle* folks from the city's South Side. And by the time you get to Kenilworth, pop. 2,500, land of United States senators and other royalty, you find yourself gawking at homes only to discover that the homes you're gawking at are the carriage houses for the real homes.

For me, it's always been a damned depressing drive.

Of course, having a lunatic with a gun in the back seat and not knowing exactly where I was headed didn't make it all the more pleasant this time around. Even though Knobby himself seemed to be enjoying the hell out of it all. Maybe, I thought, that three-houses-on-Boardwalk smile of his was because he really was from Boardwalk, and knew how out-of-place I was, myself, on this part of the board. I wondered what rent I would wind up paying, if I landed in his square?

Somewhere north of the section where they lived in mansions and a little south of the section where they built castles, Knobby told me to turn into a certain driveway—right, which is toward the lake, if you're keeping track. The driveway looked to be a half mile long.

I drive a 1971 Duster. Years of salt from the winter streets, years of bad maintenance, and just plain years have taken their toll on the body until the car looks more or less, well, like a 1971 Duster. But it runs, and runs, and runs. If I were a grizzled old prospector, it would be my loyal burro and I'd call it Old Paint, and talk to it the way Strother Martin used to talk to his donkeys in all those western movies.

Nevertheless, going down—or was it up?—that driveway I was embarrased for my old car. I doubted that such a crummy looking machine had ever blighted that particular stretch of Gold Coast road.

Knobby could have been reading my mind. *"Jee*zus, Harry. You think this road's ever seen a pile of shit like this car before?" Thank you very much.

At my crude friend's direction, I parked on an apron that would have held—and probably had held—four or five Mercedes and/or Rolls. There didn't seem much point in locking the car. I strolled behind my kidnapper toward a house that looked like it had been photographed at least once for the cover of one of those Don't You Wish You Could *Really* Live Like This? magazines.

There was no butler, which both disappointed me and satisfied my sense that life, no matter how weird it may get, is never entirely predictable. Knobby rang the bell and it was answered by a side of beef in an open yellow shirt and an ultrasuede jacket that probably was worth my month's rent. The beef was wearing no shoes—only socks, it was his house, screw you—and looked like he'd just gotten up from the couch and the morning *New York Times*. And every strand of grey hair was in place.

"Thank you, Knobby," said the tailored filet mignon. "Mr. Garnish, I am Harmon Wright."

I was once in the room—a crowded room—when a U.S. senator who everybody thought would be the next president walked in. I've never forgotten it. He didn't say a word; there were no trumpets or drums; no butler, even, spoke his name as he entered. But he hadn't come inches into the room when everybody noticed him, and everybody hushed. Here was power, and power in the flesh: the son, husband, brother, of those really in control. It was like focusing a camera. He was more there than anybody else in the room, and we all knew it.

That's how Harmon Wright looked, even standing in his doorway in stocking feet. He was more *there*—sorry, folks—than you and I would ever be.

I silently, quickly, ran through my entire stock of smart-ass opening lines, and decided on the most appropriate one.

"Hello, sir," I said, extending my hand.

He shook hands heartily—he was a strong man—and silently nodded for Knobby to bugger off. Knobby buggered off. Wright motioned for me to follow him into what I would have called the living room, but what I'm sure they had a more specialized name for. It was a big room, anyway, with no real center, just a lot of chrome and plush sofas scattered around as if a giant had gone berserk in a furniture warehouse, except all of it was somehow *placed*. There were great, full-color photographs of animals on all the available wall space. Whales, leopards, rare-looking frogs, birds whose names I couldn't even guess—a frozen zoo.

"Mr. Garnish," said Harmon Wright, sinking into a chair, "I aplogize for getting in touch with you in this fashion. But I am sure you realize that the business bringing us together is, well, *sensitive*. I trust that my man Knobby didn't cause you any undue alarm.'

He hadn't bothered to gesture for me to sit. Why was everybody lately so damned dedicated to keeping me on my feet? Anyhow, I helped myself to a mile-long sofa opposite his chair. "No problem at all, Mr. Wright," I sighed. "Guns aimed at my head and abductions outside police stations are just part of the everyday hustle for folks like me. If you ever find yourself shorthanded for thugs, though, I *do* have a telephone, and usually I even answer it."

He didn't smile. "Of course. It's only natural that you should feel angry." It wasn't an apology.

"Now," and he leaned forward, suddenly a different man, his hands fisted on his knees. "What, *exactly*, did the Skokie police want to know from you? And what, *exactly*, did you tell them?"

I could see the cords in his neck muscles. His face was red. I didn't jump at the change, but only because I've spent thirty years learning not to be surprised at the transformations people can go through. I reached in my pocket for my cigarettes, and shook one out.

"Do you mind?" I asked, the cigarette halfway to my lips.

Harmon Wright shrugged and raised his eyebrows. I assumed that meant yes, go ahead, if you must.

"Well, Mr. Wright," I said puffing. "What the police wanted to know was mainly about the shooting, last Friday, of Mrs. Marianne Healey, the wife of a man formerly engaged by you, I believe, who himself was killed last Thursday night, or maybe it was Friday morning." If I was looking for a reaction and I wasn't, I got nothing anyway.

"Yes," he said. "Fred Healey. He was running a routine security check for us, I believe. I heard. And?"

And. And I took another drag off my cigarette, looked around, and realized that there was nothing on the table in front of me that I could distinguish as an ashtray, as opposed to a valuable art nouveau teatray or T'ang Dynasty soupspoon rest. Wright really *was* a sonofabitch; he had let me light up *knowing* that it would lead to my feeling like a fool.

But I had him there: I can out-vulgar anybody in the room. I flicked a nonchalant half-inch of ash down the neck of a very valuable looking vase, and went on.

"Right. I told the cops exactly everything I know about the shooting of Marianne Healey, and the murder of Fred Healey: nothing. That's *it*. Unless you would like a verbatim report of my conversation with Inspector Carp of Skokie homicide. I don't think you would. Does that mean it's *my* turn to ask some questions?"

Harmon Wright's face relaxed into a smile. It was not a particularly nice smile. "By all means," he said. "By the way, Mr. Garnish, that vase is not to be used as an ashtray. If you need an ashtray, and, aah, I see you do, please use the flat, blue piece of porcelain directly in front of you."

"Oh. Sorry. Thanks. Now, how did you know where I would be this morning? And how did you know *why* I would be there? And why do you want to talk to me about it?"

Wright smiled again, and settled back in his expensive chair.

"I knew where you would be, Mr. Garnish, because I have some good friends in some very high places. I'm sorry if that offends your sensibilities, but that happens to be the way things are."

I shrugged. I'm always ready to accept the way things are.

"And the *why?*"

His hands began to ball into fists again, then relaxed. "The *why,* Mr. Garnish—the why is because you were seen, yesterday, meeting with *my wife*—my wife, Mr. Garnish, for lunch in the Hancock Building. And because your employer, a Miss Bridget O'Toole, of"—he paused, as if checking an address book in his head—"of O'Toole Agency, Evanston, came to see me that very afternoon. Oh, she tried very well to conceal her identity, Mr. Garnish, but it was no good, *no good.* And, finally, Mr. Garnish, I would like to know why and what the *hell* is going on here, where everyone around me is contacting police and private investigators and leaving me to feel like prime bozo."

I think it was the last thing he said that convinced me to trust him, a little. After all, nobody who describes himself as a "prime bozo" can be *all* bad. The poor little rich man, I thought, might not really have a clue to the ongoing drama. Why not give him a rundown of the story till now?

Why not, of course, was everything Yolanda Wright had told me the day before.

"Mr. Wright," I said. "I'm afraid I can't tell you much you don't already know. I met your wife because she requested that I meet her. She was concerned about Fred Healey's death. She knew from Fred that we have been good friends, and she called to see if I could give her any information about—it. I couldn't. My boss, Bridget O'Toole, visited you because she thought it would be worth the trouble to establish a business connection with you. The private eye gig isn't really thriving these days, you know?" I cast a hopeful, cringing smile at him and felt it wither and die before it got to his eyes. I went on.

"See, she had heard from me that Fred was doing some work for you folks at Ecology International—I don't know what, but some work—and I guess she just figured she might as well get her name on your address book. You *are* a pretty well-known man, sir."

I thought it was a hell of a performance. I had managed to sound concerned with the Wright fame, name, and fortune, ignorant about the hunk of coke Fred was supposed to have scarfed up for some hidden purpose, and yet smart enough—*just* smart enough, like a kennel-raised and housebroken weasel—to be able to absorb and handle a little more confidential information about whatever was *really* wrong *chez* Wright.

That's what I thought. Harmon Wright, I guess, didn't have the same idea.

"You snotty little son of a *bitch!*" he shouted, rising to his feet. "Don't you play games with *me,* you little fucker. Do you think I'm a fool? Do you think I'm just *anybody?* Don't you know what I can do to you, if I want to have it done?"

I was impressed. "Yes, sir, I do," I said. I was beginning to wonder if I'd have to fight my way out of the place. It looked harder to get out of than Ryan's Pub. "Believe me, I don't want any trouble with you. I've told you what I think—what I *think,* mind you—is the truth. And I'm sorry if it all sounds like a scam, but it's what I know." I don't claim to be good at much, but lying under pressure is among my best things.

It didn't work. Wright was out of control, over the line, call it what you like. And it scared the hell out of me. I've looked in the face of real despair, real craziness, a couple of times in my life. And every time I do, I hope I never have to again.

"What you *know,*" he whispered, and his whisper was worse than his shout. "What you *know!* What the goddamned Jesus H. Christ hell could you, you wretched little piece of shit, *know?*" He was pacing back and forth across his, I figured, very expensive carpet, and he had picked up the art object I'd mistaken for an ashtray, and he was rubbing it—no, really, rubbing it—as he paced and talked.

"Do you *know* what it's like to live a life of absolute—of absolute—do you know, you little bastard, what real fear is? Do you know how hard it is to be—to be married to a woman who, who, oh, Christ!"

And as he said that he threw the vase, or ashtray, or whatever the hell it was, against the wall facing him. He threw it as hard as he could have, and I ducked; I've got this thing about my eyes, see.

I guess that helped him. At least, he sank down on the chair again, looking like he'd just worked out at the gym for an hour. And, oddly enough, he seemed not to remember how crazy he'd been a minute before, I didn't think it was my place to remind him.

"Well. Right." He was panting. "Sorry if I was—was overbearing," and he laughed. "It's only that I really have been under some special strain the last few days. Listen, would you join me in a drink?"

By now you know I'm not about to march in the next temperance crusade down Michigan Avenue. But I was also not damn likely to let somebody—even somebody who could buy and sell me and all the other Garnishes before brunch—get away with believing a shot of expensive Scotch made it O.K. to talk to me like I was something he had found under his shoe after a long walk in the woods.

"No, thanks," I said, my mouth so dry my tongue clicked against the palate. "Go ahead yourself, though."

He rose again, slower this time, and made his way to the bar caddy where he helped himself to a very large bourbon and soda. When he turned back to me, he was smiling the same placid smile with which he had greeted me. The only difference was that now I knew I was dealing with a madman.

"Look, Harry—may I call you Harry?—*good*. Look, Harry, there's no need for us to quarrel about this thing. I *know* my wife is hiding something from me. Oh, hell, I don't know what it is, maybe she's got a lover or maybe she's become a Buddhist. I don't care. I love Yolanda, and she knows it, and she knows that nothing she could do would ever interfere with that love. It's an unchangeable thing, like—"his glance swept around the photographs of endangered animals on his walls—"like nature itself, do you know?"

I didn't know. I thought the whole point of the thing was that nature did change. But it didn't seem the time for a refresher course in evolution. I nodded.

"So, you see, Harry," he went on, "all I want from you is some clue about what's been bothering her lately. And, of course, what it all has to do with the murder of Mr. Healey. Really, I only want to know these things so I can help her. Believe that."

I did. Just the same way I had believed Yolanda Wright when she'd said, "He's my husband—I love him." The man before me was a bully, a rich and arrogant bastard who knew exactly what he could buy and wasn't the least bit bothered about buying it, and he was probably also crazy. But he also loved his lady, and his lady loved him. That's no citation for a Congressional Medal of Honor, I know. But it's a little better than the stride a lot of us manage to hit.

I was trying really hard to dislike the guy, and he kept giving me the damndest reasons not to. It was frustrating.

I lit another cigarette, now that I knew where the ashtray was. "Mr. Wright," I said, "honest to God, if there was anything I could tell you to set your mind at rest, I would. But there just isn't. What I told you before is, really—believe *me*—all I can tell you. Now," I smiled, "you can have my legs broken or whatever, but that's all I know. Sorry to be a disappointment."

He sighed, shook his head, smiled, and dammit, I felt like I had let him down.

"All right. Perhaps it was a mistake on my part to bring you here at all. I will make it worth your while, of course. Is two hundred dollars reasonable as a, say, consulting fee? Not that you need mention it to your employer or anyone else, you know."

Two hundred was fine, if only I knew what I was really getting paid for. But even if I didn't, it was still fine. I told me so, he fished in his wallet, and handed me four fiftys.

"Good," he said. "Of course, Harry, that two hundred is also to keep very quiet about Ecology International. I'm sure I can trust you, since I know I can buy you." I jerked my head. It was like a whiplash, and his eyes were glinting with the knowledge that he'd aimed it just right.

"No doubt," he continued smoothly, "the police will discover who killed Healey"—he wasn't Mr. Healey anymore, I noticed, now that I'd taken the cash—"and I'm quite sure it will turn out to have nothing to do with E.I. or—or Yolanda or me. Now, just a moment," he said, picking up the phone and punching a two-digit, in-house number. "Yes, Knobby. Will you please come to the entrance and take Mr. Garnish back to his car?"

Knobby was there when the front door opened. Wright didn't take my hand. Instead he stared at me for a moment, husked, "I'm counting on you, Harry," turned on his heel, and stalked back into the house, leaving the door to swing shut by itself. I might as well have been delivering a rhinestone collar for his cat. If he had a cat.

"I'll be seeing you, Harry," grinned Knobby, nastily, as I pried open the door of my Duster. But enough was enough. I didn't have to serve as cat litter for the whole planet, I figured.

"Fine with me, Knob," I said, and then paused, getting into my car. "Only remember, Red, I didn't fix your clock with your boss in there by telling him you've been running errands on the side for his old lady."

It was partly a guess, but it worked. He went redder, then paler, then looked me in the eye and shrugged. "Yeah, well, maybe that *is* something to think about. O.K., boopsie, clear out."

In twenty-four hours, I reflected as I squeegeed down the drive back to Sheridan Road, I'd been kidnapped twice, insulted by a cop, and had met at least one certifiable nut. I was tired, and I still didn't have Fred's famous package.

I headed for O'Toole Agency's offices. My three tailing operations still needed seeing to; I hadn't been in touch with my snitches since the morning Fred died. I still had one can of ale, I thought, in the office refrigerator. And today, being Tuesday, wasn't, thank God, doughnut day.

The hell with Fred Healey. The hell with everybody.

• 12

As FAR as I could see, the trail was cold, and getting colder every minute. If Carp had really had anything to go on in Fred's murder, he would have been a lot more primitive with me. I knew, from sad experience, how primitive Carp could be when the mood was on him and he knew he had the leverage. And if Carp and the Skokie P.D. didn't have anything to work with, then nobody did. Something like eighty percent of all killings are solved within five square miles of their commission—you can look it up. The major exceptions are mass killers ("God told me to do it through secret messages in the daily headlines") who are just irrational enough to be clever; kinky killers ("There I was, there she was, and I thought, why not?") who do one perfectly horrible, insane thing and then plunge back into the ocean of normality; and professionals. The professionals are so neat and so specialized in their range of victims that everybody except the FBI just leaves them alone.

Such were my thoughts as I parked a block or two south of O'Toole Agency and trudged to my office. Fred Healey was dead, and nothing would bring him back to life. His widow and his kid— somebody's kid, anyhow—were very much alive and might be very approachable. I could imagine worse fates than becoming the father of Fred, Jr., living in something like bliss with Marianne (she really was dynamite in bed), and growing old as gracefully as possible while I waited for Bridget to clear out and make Harry Garnish Investigations, Inc. a splendid reality.

And maybe, too elephants would start to shit diamonds.

Before I braved the office, I decided to have a visit and a chat with Ben Gross, president and general manager of Ben Gross Dry Cleaners, Inc.

Ben, by the way, is probably the worst dry cleaner in Chicago.

He loses clothes a lot, he over- or under-charges all the time, and he generally doesn't give a healthy rat's ass about the business of running a dry cleaning business.

He's a mathematician, you see. Or he *was* a mathematician, in Germany in the 'thirties, until one day the Nazis came to his office at the university and carted him away and spent the next six years doing very ugly things to him, because he wasn't only a mathematician, he was also a Jew. O.K., O.K., I know: It's an old story and you've heard it before. It's just that Ben is the one guy I *know* who went through it. And sometimes, when I run out of other things to be depressed about, I get depressed about the fact that Dr. Benjamin Gross, from the time he was sprung from Treblinka until the time you're reading this, has run a second-rate dry cleaner's shop in Evanston, and has never opened another math book.

As usual there was no business in the shop. As usual there was a samovar steaming. And as usual, Ben was reading. Today's book, I noticed, was something called *Gödel*, *Escher*, *Bach*. Seemed like a dumb title to me.

"Harry!" he said as soon as I came into the shop. "Good to see you! You want a cup of tea?"

We sat behind the counter an I fished out two cigarettes. Ben gave up smoking years ago, so he only smokes the ones I give him. We puffed, sipped, and stared at nothing in particular.

"So, Harry," Ben finally said, "you're awful quiet today. No jokes, no nothing. What is it, my friend? You got worries, maybe?"

I took a drag of my cigarette and a sip of Ben's godawful tea. "No worries, Ben," I said. "I guess I'm just down, you know?"

Ben set down his cup. "Listen, Harry," he said. "Nobody is *just down*. That's the kind of bullshit, you leave it for the idiots of the world—there's plenty, trust me—to say. You're down, you're down *for a reason*. You don't want to talk about it, fine. But don't, Harry, tell me you're *just down*. It's your friend Mr. Healey, maybe?"

Maybe it was. Maybe it was what my friend, Mr. Healey, had left behind. And maybe it was something else altogether, something I couldn't quite find a name for. Ben and I talked about it for a half-hour, and couldn't make any more sense of what was bugging me than when I'd come in. And if Ben couldn't make sense of it, I figured, then nobody could.

See, I'm a lucky man. The rich have to pay for their analysts; all I have to do is drink tea.

Ben did say one interesting thing. Or rather, he did one interesting thing. As I was rambling on about everything that had happened to me so far, he jerked his head curiously when I mentioned Harmon Wright.

"Harmon Wright?" he said. "The grocery store Harmon Wright?"

"Yeah," I said. "You know something about him?"

He shook his head. "No. No. Only, only rumors. But, Harry"—and he shivered, one of the only times I've seen him do that—"Harry, if you can help it, don't mess with that man, all right?"

I finished my tea, said *shalom* to Ben (he always winces when I do that), and went up to O'Toole Agency.

Brenda, fat Brenda, was on duty at the phone when I walked in, even though it was after lunch—time for her to be taking her daily nap—and she seemed to be having a difficult time focusing her eyes and getting her fingers to hit the right buttons on the phones. I would keep her on, I thought, after Bridget left and I married Marianne and took things over. It would be the *right* thing to do; the lordly gesture of the new prince, retaining the serfs who had tilled the baron's soil so long and with such little fruit.

"Hi, Brenda," I said. "Any messages?"

She shook her head and went back to staring at the phone as if it was a strange visitor from another world.

Or maybe, I thought, I would fire her ass.

I made my way to my office, passing Bridget's mini rain forest. And once I got inside I closed the door with a feeling of relief. It was like coming home, to a place I knew, even if I didn't like it. Four blank walls, but by God they were *my* blank walls.

And then I groaned. Bridget's door had been ajar as I'd passed it. Nobody home but old Phil, who had looked at me sadly, all five of his stupid splayed faces leaning on the sofa, turned toward me, and yellowing. In the confusion of the last few days I supposed nobody had watered him.

I sighed, heaved myself out of my chair, and went back to fetch the plastic container that is our all-purpose watering can from under Brenda's desk. I filled it from the tap in the john and carried it carefully back to Bridget's office.

"There you go, Phil," I said as I poured into the artificial dirt in his pot. "Skoal." After a while a tiny trickle ran out from an undiscoverable crack. Phil had had his fill. Somebody was happy, anyway. And now I could get back to what I called, in my gayer moods, work.

I had gotten in touch with the snitches working Mr. Gray and Mr. Brown, and the snitch working Mrs. Wysocki, was, his answering service told me, not available. Since when, I wondered, do burnt-out rumdums with no talents but dirty minds afford answering services? Is that what inflation really means? Anyway, it felt good to be back at work again after the interruption of the last few days. Here I was again, hot on the trail of seedy infidelities and sleazy betrayals, backed up by a platoon of camera-laden creeps, with minimum risk to life or limb.

It was such a *safe* life. Why had Fred stepped outside the borders? Oh, yes, he said on the tape that there was big money involved, that there was a provision for his son (*his* son—Had he really believed that? I hoped so), that there was an insurance policy. Well, maybe so, maybe so.

Fred had been a *good* friend, a *nice* guy. I don't know, maybe he was the only friend I had that I could really talk to about things that mattered to both of us. And I had cheated him the worst way you can cheat a friend, and he had known it. Fine. So. I had run his stupid errands for him, and it had all come up zero, zero, zero, as I could have told him if he'd asked me.

But he hadn't asked me. He hadn't asked me because I was screwing his wife and still meeting him on the street with a big smile and asking him to pop around the corner for a beer. Fred was always the romantic. He would have taken something like that hard.

Funny, but sitting alone in my office watching my last can of ale get warm in my hands, I finally felt that my friend was dead. "I'm *dead*," he had said on the tape, and it hadn't meant a lot to me except a pause in a message I was supposed to, somehow, act on. But now I shared Fred's surprise and shock at the simple, the bare, the blank fact. We had laughed at one another across a lot of bar tables, slapped one another on the back after a lot of ridiculous behavior, acted stupid the way only good friends act stupid in one another's company. And now that was all over.

I had done enough. My eyes were stinging, but I knew I was a nice man. I ran errands for dead people, I obstructed evidence for bed partners, I wept for friends, I fed thirsty philodendrons: I was just entirely O.K.

And there was new business.

My phone buzzed and lit up, and I picked it up to hear the buzzed and lit-up voice of Brenda. "Harry? There's a Mr.—a Mr. Cacciatore here who would like to consult with someone about an investigation. Can you see him?"

Mr. Cacciatore? Come *on*, I thought to myself. A joke name for a gangster in a high school skit? Did his friends call him "Chicken" for short? But then, I thought, somebody had to bear the name. It was a real name, and, I remembered, it meant "hunter" in Italian.

"Right, Brenda. Show him in, would you, please?"

A new client at O'Toole Agency isn't exactly a cause for universal rejoicing—we don't break out the champagne every time a fresh victim of mopery or mugging shambles into the reception room—but it isn't, either, an event we fail to take into account. I straightened my tie, quickly checked the office for empty beer cans or unemptied ash trays, and by the time Brenda knocked on my door, had the place looking sterile and serviceable.

Mr. Cacciatore, if Cacciatore was his name, would probably never have been called "Chicken" in grammar school. He was large, very large. I'm about medium height, myself—5'7" if you must know, though some of my best friends have told me I look smaller than that, a natural sneak. Cacciatore, in a red turtleneck and an overcoat that must have orphaned hundreds of tiny animals, charged through the door and immediatley filled the office. He had the face and aura of a sensitive truck driver, and you could almost hear the air ripple as he moved his arms.

"Mr. O'Toole," he said, sitting in the chair on the other side of my desk without being asked.

He was client one thousand to say that. "Mr. Garnish," I said.

"Miss O'Toole, or Ms. O'Toole, if you prefer, runs the agency, but I am sort of the chief of operations." I was sort of the only other person working at the agency, but "chief of operations" sounded nicer. "Now, Mr. Cacciatore, what is it you think we can do for you?"

At this point, usually, prospective clients begin to babble. "Well, you know, I've never really been to a private detective before, but you see, my wife lately . . ." or, "my husband lately . . ." or, "a very trusted employee of mine lately . . . ." (Those last ones are the ones you watch for: not as juicy as the others if you're in the business for cheap thrills, but a helluva lot more profitable, on the average.) And like, I guess, priests in the confessional, you get into the habit of letting them babble for a while until they're babbled out and ready, finally, to tell you what's really bugging them and what you're supposed fix.

My new friend the grim grey giant wasn't having any, though. "I want you to meet a man for me, Mr. O'Toole. I want you to take what that man is going to hand you, deliver it to this address"—he flipped an index card with some writing on it onto my desk—" and then forget that you ever talked to me. For this I will give you five hundred dollars in advance and another fifteen hundred when the delivery has been made and checked. This isn't breaking any law, it doesn't involve any risk to you or whoever you send, and if you don't want to do it I won't contact you again, and I can always find somebody else who will. Now. Yes or No?"

I tried to widen my eyes and look confused. Not that I wasn't confused, but I thought if I could convince him that I really thought he *was* the tooth fairy come back to earth, he might get confident enough to tell me a little more of what this was really all about.

"Uh—it's Garnish, not O'Toole. Garnish. And do you mind my asking what this man is going to hand me, and how you picked me for this honor?"

His face—and his face was as big as the rest of him—relaxed into a smile. He had the hook in, had felt the tug, and now he just had to relax and turn the reel slowly, slowly. "I'm supposed to get a yes or no from you," he said, "nothing else. But, sure, Mr.—*Garnish*—I can tell you a little more. What you're going to get is an envelope, and inside the envelope is a notarized, signed statement. Okay?"

"Not okay," I said. "You're offering me two k. to be an accessory after the fact to blackmail, aren't you?" I figured Cacciatore for a seasoned fisherman, which meant he wouldn't trust a fish that didn't at least try to sound. And if he did give me any more line, it meant that he really wanted *me*, not just anybody to run his errand.

He bit. The smile froze, he looked exasperated, but he didn't get up. "Look, Garnish, I *told* you I can always get somebody else to do this for me. But—aah, bullshit—it *isn't* blackmail. I work for a national news magazine, okay? I won't tell you its name, because if this all goes through, you'll know soon enough who we are. My rag is preparing a piece on charity scams—*very* big buck causes that are really cover operations for some nasty goings-on. What you're picking up is a statement by one of the employees of one of those scams, and you're delivering it to an undercover reporter who's getting the goods on that particular operation. Now that's a hell of a lot more than you should know, and I'm only telling you because if you even think about blowing the operation—opening the envelope, contacting the scam, whatever—we can dry your ass six ways from Sunday and make you part of the story when it breaks, too. Now," he reached in his jacket pocket and took out a business envelope which he tossed across the desk to me. It contained five well-used and crumpled hundred dollar bills. "Do we deal or don't we? I don't have all day."

"So why don't you meet the guy yourself?" I asked.

He stared at me like I'd suggested he fart at the Queen's dinner table. "Damn!" he said. "Didn't you ever hear of undercover journalism?"

Well, I hadn't, in fact. But then the total tonnage of what I hadn't heard of could feed Asia.

I didn't like it at all. He'd avoided telling me how he picked me in the first place, which was a sure indication that I was targeted for something. If his story was the truth, then I had the uncomfortable feeling that Ecology International might be one of the scams involved in the exposé. But if that were the case, why would Cacciatore tell me a half-truth that was bound to alert me to the possible connection, and the sure risk to my own admittedly ordinary but by me well-loved ass? I sighed a private sigh for the good old days, when liars *were* liars.

"We deal," I said. "Where's the drop?"

"Northwestern University campus," he said. "Do you know where University Hall is?"

I didn't, offhand. But I assured him I could probably discover its whereabouts. I was a detective, wasn't I?

"Okay. Right out in front of University Hall, there's a big rock. Don't ask me why it's there—some damn dumb university tradition, college boy bullshit." Not a college boy, I reflected. Well, neither was I. "Anyhow, between nine-thirty and ten tonight, somebody is going to be standing by the rock. Somebody who won't look like a student." He grinned.

"You?"

"Uh-uh. You're not going to see me again. At least not if you do what you're supposed to. What you do—and closer to nine-thirty, he's going to be freezing his butt off—is locate the guy, walk up to him, and say, 'Cold as a witch's tit, ain't it?' Just say that. He'll laugh, say, 'I wouldn't know, I've never had a witch.' If he don't say that, he isn't your man. Then you offer him a cigarette—oh, you smoke?"

"A lot," I said.

"Good. Make sure you have some with you. Just hold the pack out to him, don't say anything. He'll take a cigarette, and slip you the envelope, and split. You split then, deliver the envelope to that address"—his banana-finger tapped the index card on my desk—" and then you go home, get a good night's sleep, and next day, tomorrow, you'll find fifteen hundred more of those little suckers you're holding making a nest in your mailbox here."

Now I've seen my share of James Bond movies. I know all about signs and countersigns and stuff like that, and I also know—sometimes—when somebody's pulling my chain. I was pretty sure this was one of those times. But in spite of myself I was getting fascinated, not only with *who* would think I was dumb enough to play secret agent man for more than my month's salary, but also with *why* they thought I was that dumb. Had somebody been going over my high school grades again? Anyway, the only way to find out was to *be* that dumb. I nodded at Cacciatore.

"Right," I said. "And since you like paying in used bills, why don't you make the next delivery to my home mailbox? I'm sure you can find my address, and there's no need to bother my boss, Miss O'Toole, that is, about all this."

He smiled again, landed, hung, and all but scaled. "Sure thing, Garnish. I'll make a note of it. About nine-thirty, then?"

He rose and we shook hands, just two weasels out on a spree. He shrugged his big fur coat back on and paraded out of the office. I glanced at the address on the index card for the first time. No name, just an apartment number in Sandburg Village, the hip high-rent complex on the North Side.

It didn't matter. I knew I'd keep the appointment, and I also knew I'd never get to the address on the card. Maybe because I wouldn't have to, maybe because I wouldn't be able to. Someone, I was sure, wanted to give me much more than an envelope. Someone wanted to impress something on me. I was pretty sure that what they wanted to impress had to do with Fred Healey, Harmon Wright and Ecology International. The only problem was how strenuously they wanted to impress it.

Call me psychic.

• 13

Now, I had some options. I could call my buddy Clarence Carp and tell him that, if he wanted some more information about Fred's murder, he could stroll by the famous Northwestern U. rock tonight and have a chat. But to do that I would have to admit that I knew more about the whole affair than I had let on to him in the first place. And that was likely to get Clarence miffed. And Clarence miffed was something I didn't need to see.

I could walk to the office next door and tell Bridget, if she was back, that somebody was trying to set me, or her, or both of us, up for some heavy nastiness, and that it all had something—God knew what—to do with the death of poor Fred. But to do that would involve Bridget in the nastiness, and if I knew her at all, I knew that she would take it more personally—and further—than I wanted to.

I could take the five hundred in cash, take out the money in my savings account, drag Marianne from her convalescent bed, and fly her, me, and Fred, Jr. to St. Thomas where I could open a beachcomber's bar. I'd water the rum, Marianne would fry the hamburgers, and the kid could learn to belly surf.

Or I could keep the appointment.

So, I don't know what you do in situations of maximum moral stress (that's the way, believe me, my boss would put it). But what I do is, I look for a way out.

I decided to call Harmon Wright.

It was early afternoon by the time Cacciatore left, so I had plenty of day ahead before going to meet my appointment and; as far as I knew, having the Mormon Tabernacle Choir do a fla-menco on my liver. Of course, I didn't know that there was any connection between Cacciatore's errand and the business of the Wrights and Fred—didn't know, except the way you know a bloody sunrise means a rainy day tomorrow. What's the old saying? "Red sky at morning, sailors take warning." Well, a sailor I never was; can't even swim. But I've gotten my balls caught in the wringer often enough by *not* heeding those old sayings and signals; and these days I'm just too old and breakable to ignore them any more.

So I called Harmon Wright. Don't tell me what you're thinking. You're thinking, "Jesus, this guy goes to a hell of a lot of trouble not to explain why he does what he does." And you're right. Well I was getting very scared. And, as often as I have been scared, I never like to admit it. You see, I knew I would wind up keeping my appointment at the Northwestern rock that night. For practical reasons. Dig it, I've got a low pain threshhold. I cancel one dentist appointment out of three, and I *hate* it when people step on my face. But I hate it even worse when people get *their* faces stepped on because of me. Mind you, it doesn't hurt as much at the beginning. But—especially if it's a friend who's been face-danced—the pain tends to last a lot longer.

So, for the third time, and this time you get the whole enchilada: I called Harmon Wright. Because I was plenty scared. To see if he could get me off the hook.

Fat freaking chance.

He wasn't at his home, or at least the guy answering his phone said he wasn't after I'd given my name. So I called his office, wondering if I'd get a bugger-off response there, too. And I damn near got one. The secretary on the other end of the line took my name, switched off for a whole minute, and then came back with a surprise.

"Mr. Wright requests that you call him on his private line, Mr. Garnish," she said, and I could almost hear the puzzlement that must have been on her face. I guess usually only presidents, senators, and harp seals got to use the private line of Ecology International. And maybe some of her puzzlement rubbed off because when she gave me Wright's private number, I realized—for the first time, honest—that I might have sat down at a game where I couldn't even raise the ante. And by then—I was dialling the phone—it was too late. Isn't it always?

"Yes, Mr. Garnish?" came Wright's voice over the phone.

I don't know if you've ever called the gas company about your bill, or called the bank that just sent you a notice of three bounced checks in your account. But if you have, then you've got some sense of the tone—I'm talking zero degrees Kelvin—of Wright's voice. Three words, and every trace of the hysterical bastard who'd nearly put out my eye, just a few hours ago, was gone. I swear to God, I almost came to attention.

"Uh, yes, sir," I garbled. "Sorry to bother you at your, your private number, sir. I know you must be awfully busy." (Busy doing what, I thought, Garnish, you dumb shit? Saving whales? Teaching whooping cranes to breed?)

Mercifully he interrupted me. "That's all right, Garnish. You know, I'm afraid I may have been a little, well, a little *harsh* with you this morning. I'm sure you'll be kind enough to accept my apology."

Yessir. When you're worth the net price of a fleet of 747's and the annual electric bill of three Balkan city states, that's one thing you can always be sure of: people will accept your apologies. Oh, *excuse* me, was that your sofa I crapped on? Awfully sorry, you know.

I accepted his apology.

"So," he said. "What is it?" Not, "What can I do for you?" Not even, "What do you want?" Nope. Just like I'd brought a llama-load of tribute from the tribes of outer Brazil (if there is an outer Brazil): "What is it?"

"Well, sir," I said, "what it is, is that I've been thinking about our conversation earlier today, and I wonder if maybe we shouldn't clear up some things before we, uh, go further, you know?"

"Yes?" His tone was exactly what that stupid opening deserved.

"Yes. Can you tell me, sir, if you're aware of any investigations of E.I.'s finances by, aah, by news people of any sort? I mean, has anyone from the press asked you about your books lately?"

The answer was immediate, and maybe even a little too immediate, as if he'd been expecting just that question.

"No. Absolutely not. You know, of course, that any organization like E.I. is under constant scrutiny, even under constant threat of innuendo, constant danger of irresponsible whispers and petty carping by people who can't believe that an organization can simply want to do *good*. *I* know that, Mr. Garnish, and I have protected E.I. from the jackals. What do they call it? 'Investigative reporting,' that's what they call it, and what is it? It's jackals snapping at the nearest shreds of flesh, that's what it is."

"Yessir, but—"

"But nothing. Watergate was the beginning, and let me tell you, Garnish, it was a bad thing for the country. You think Nixon was a bad man, a bad leader? Could anyone else have gotten out of Vietnam with honor? Could anyone else have opened trade— very important trade, I might add—with China without being called a pinko? And what did they do to him, those 'investigative reporters?' "

I was about to say that they had revealed that our lad had violated the Constitution six ways from Sunday and made private rights a bad joke, but then I remembered two things. The first was that Harmon Wright, as far as I knew, didn't give a rat's ass about private rights anyhow. The second was that he was hiring me, not the other way around. I let him go on.

"And Ted Kennedy, and Jerry Brown, and—and John DeLorean, all the same, all the same sad story. Men of vision brought down by the jackals. All of them, Garnish, men who might have made a difference, men who might have meant something more to the world than just another boring entry in the obituary column. And what happened to all of them? Brought down . . . brought down. I can tell you this: E.I. and what it stands for is not going to go into the dark because of the jackals. No. We are trying to save the *earth*, dammit. And no fucking newspaper is going to get in the way of that."

Well, damn all. The way he said, "We are trying to save the *earth*," I could almost believe he was Flash Gordon; at least he had a very severe Buster Crabbe syndrome. Anyway, I'd found out what I wanted to find out. Harmon Wright had no connection with the guy who was supposed to meet me that night. I mean, nobody gets that crazy or that passionate when they're trying to tell a really good lie. And if Wright's first response to my first question had seemed prepared, a little too immediate, it wasn't because he had been expecting it from me; it was because he had been asking it to himself, probably for a long time.

"Yessir," I said. "Thank you, sir. I just wanted to make sure . . ."

"Don't bother with explanations, Harry," he barked (and I made a mental note that, at least, he remembered my first name). "I agreed to speak with you because I assumed you had something important to tell me. That was a wrong assumption, as it appears. If you can discover anything about my—wife's—involvement in this mess, please let me know. Otherwise, do not communicate with me again."

Like that. Just like that, the receiver clicked down on the other end of the line, and I was left no more or less confused than before I'd called the bastard.

So, at the price of some humiliation, I'd found out that H. Wright didn't know he was being investigated, or didn't want me to know he was being investigated, or wasn't being investigated, or, as far as I knew, really *was* going to save the earth. I just knew, as I hung up the phone, that I was going, God help me, to keep my appointment that night.

I toasted myself for my splendid moral sense and began dialling the number of my one outstanding snitch. I couldn't wait to hear what Mrs. Wysocki had been up to since the last installment. Mr. Wysocki was due to check in at the end of the week for a progress report, and I wanted to be sure we gave him enough reading to fill up his evenings, since there didn't seem to be much else available to him in that line.

I was in luck. My man was back home. I was in the middle of an engaging, eye-witness account of some Saturday afternoon, Olympic-class hijinks in a Lake Forest motel (buckle *down,* Wysocki!) when there was a knock on my door.

"Great work, Ernie," I interrupted my storyteller. "Look, I have to get off now. Just make sure you've got the dates and the photos all together by Thursday, and drop them off here, okay?"

Ernie said that would be no problem, no problem at all, and rang off. I hung up and shouted, "Come in," and watched Bridget O'Toole wade into my office and sink into the nearest chair.

It's a rare event when Bridget comes into my office. I think it offends her. My office, that is. When she first came here for me to work for her and dash my hopes of finally having my own, my very own business, she took one look at the spare, bare walls of my office and the next day came in with two prints—landscapes with castles and sheep and things, they were—that she said were suitable for framing and that she thought might cheer up the place.

The prints are still in my office. I've never had them framed or hung, they're standing on edge, there, between the wall and my filing cabinet. I don't like landscapes, okay? They remind me of all the places I've never been.

If it's rare that Bridget comes into my office, though, it's rarer still that she looks as bothered as she did when she came in this time.

"Bridget," I said. "What is it?"

She stared at me, an odd sort of stare, before she answered. She wasn't dressed, I noticed, in the orange circus tent contraption of yesterday. She was wearing a black and white sort of suit that reminded me, in its austerity, of her convent past. I had never seen her dress like that. Even the Church, if I wasn't mistaken, had declared by the time she left the convent that nuns were allowed to dress like normal female human beings—a dazzling leap from the sixteenth to the nineteenth century. I wondered if she was reverting.

"Harry," she said. "I'm afraid we've stumbled onto something too big for us to handle. And I want you to tell me if you think so, too. Do you know what Gödel's theorem is?"

She always does that. I mean, if there's a roundabout way to find your path to the center of the maze, if there's a difficult way to solve the equation, if there's a hard fingering for the chord on the piano, then good old Bridget will find it for you. And then she'll explain why the roundabout way is the only one that really works. Girdle's theorem, for Christ's sweet sake.

I lit a cigarette and wished there was more ale. "Well, no, Bridget, now that you mention it, I don't think I can say what Girdle's theorem is. Doesn't have anything to do with Occam's razor, does it? I know *that*," I said proudly.

She didn't smile. That always meant there was a lecture inside her screaming to get out. "No, no, Harry, not *girdle*. *Gödel, Kurt* Gödel. A brilliant early twentieth-century mathematician. You see, I taught number theory for a few years, it was in Philadelphia, Gödel has always fascinated me. What he argued, well, *proved,* really, is that any closed system, no matter how perfect or how perfectly closed, would always produce propositions, conclusions, facts that were both obviously true and yet that could *not* be proved from the axioms, the elementary propositions, of the system itself. My goodness, what a mind he must have had!" She sighed.

I didn't sigh. "My God, that's just amazing, Bridget," I said. "Listen, I can't wait to share this news with my friends. I know at least five or six guys whose lives this kind of stuff might change. *Girdle's* theorem, you say? Let me make a note of it real quick. Yessir, I can see how this is going to save me a hell of a lot of trouble and time from now on."

I was a man, remember, who had already decided that I was going to drive four miles to get beaten up that night. It had a distinct influence on my interest in number theory.

"Oh, Harry, I'm sorry," smiled my ugly boss. "I know how silly all this must sound to you, knowing as much as you do about the business, and everything," she paused, waiting, I guess, for a polite denial. Damned if I was going to give her one. "But, you know," she continued, "all *I* really know about—about things—is what I learned from you, dear, and what I learned, well, what I learned *before.*"

Before, of course, meant before her old man had had the wiring in his brain short out; before she felt forced to leave the life she'd chosen and probably loved for thirty years; before she had to rely on Brenda's boozy inefficiency and my radiant charm and goodwill for companionship. All of a sudden I felt like saying something nice to her. But the moment for that had passed, at least this time around.

"You see," she went on, "Godel's theorem is so exciting, dear, because though it *seems* to refer just to mathematics, it actually refers to *reality itself.* Any closed system isn't, *can't* be a truly closed system! Reality isn't logical. It—it *leaks,* you know! Leaks into places, into other realities, that we wouldn't have suspected in the first place. Yes, dear, you were right. It does, after all, have something to do with Occam's razor. In a bitter sort of way. Occam tells us that the simplest answer always answers even the most complicated problem. But Gödel tells us that the simplest answer is never, can never be, as simple as we would like it to be."

Despite myself, I was getting fascinated. It all sounded like something I'd heard or thought before. But where?

"Fine, Bridget," I said. "That's all really good to know. But is there any reason you decided to share the big news with me just now?"

"Oh! Yes, of course. Sorry, Harry, I'm afraid I'm becoming absentminded. Well, anyhow, dear, I just wonder if we shouldn't return Mrs. Wright's money to her and withdraw from the case."

The revelation of Gödel's theorem hadn't really surprised me; I'd always suspected that reality was trickier than they wanted you to find out. But this did. Bridget O'Toole actually wanted to back out of an impossible, intolerable situation? Damn? Old Gödel must have had more on the ball than I thought.

Never mind that I had almost forgotten that Yolanda Wright was our client of record in this whole thing. And that this might be an honorable way of backing out of an appointment I didn't especially want to keep, that evening.

"Well, golly, Bridget," I said. "That sure is an interesting idea, especially coming from you. Mind telling me how you came by it?" I was trying to do my Walter Brennan, oh-shucks old prospector voice. Nobody ever notices.

"As I said, dear, Gödel's theorem. And I have just spoken with Clyde Crews." She looked at me in triumph. I looked at her the way a sheep looks at a 747.

"Right. You talked to Clyde Crews. Who's he, anyway, a friend of this guy Girdle?"

"Oh, Harry, *please*. Clyde Crews is the man to whom, according to Mrs. Wright, the packages of cocaine was addressed, care of Ecology International. I've had a meeting with him, in the coffee shop across from the Hancock Building. I arranged it all this morning," she added with a touch of pride I could call "girlish," if the adjective weren't so completely inappropriate to anything to do with Bridget O'Toole.

"Swell. So Clyde *told* you about Girdle, and then you decided to drop the case," I said. I mean, once I make up my mind to be stupid, I never look back.

Bridget didn't even rise to the bait. "Mr. Crews," she went on, "is a very soft-spoken, polite man. He joined E.I., as they call it, because, he says, he really believes in the cause of conservation, and because he is really committed to trying to save the endangered species of this planet. He says he was in the Peace Corps, in Colombia, when he was younger, and that it was the work he did there that led him to join E.I. last year."

"And?"

"And he is a liar. He became disturbed when I asked him about any unauthorized mailings to E.I. from South America. Not that I actually asked him about the cocaine Mrs. Wright claims to have discovered, mind you. But as soon as I asked him if they ever received any packages or letters that they hadn't expected, he became very nervous, told me that they carefully monitored all their overseas communications, and asked me what it was I wanted to know."

"I'm not surprised. How the hell did you contact him in the first place?"

"Oh, that was no problem. I identified myself as Sister Juanita, from a national catholic magazine, and told the office that I had been asked to contact Mr. Crews for an interview about the good work of Ecology International."

I was about to laugh appreciatively at the joke, and then I caught a glimpse of her eyes. It wasn't funny. Dammit, she *was* Sister Juanita—or had been. And probably still wished she was. The urge to say something nice came back. She hadn't had to use that particular story, or that particular name. But she had. She was dumpy, she didn't understand a lot of things, and she could be a giant pain in the ass. But she was tough, tough in ways, maybe, that I didn't even understand. But I could respect it.

"So what went down?" I asked, leaning back in my chair. I think it was the first time I really spoke to her as if she were in the same business.

"What went down," she smiled, "is that Mr. Crews is up to something. He wasn't in the Peace Corps as a young man. I was, as a middle-aged nun, and I learned enough from our conversation to tell that he was lying about *that*. And why would he volunteer an irrelevant lie unless he also had a relevant one to tell?"

"I think you'd better go on," I said.

"Yes. Well, you see, when I asked him—very innocently, as you know I can—if there was a connection between E.I. and the State Department, he looked at me as if it was a combination no one had ever thought of before!"

I was losing the ball again. "Uh, Bridget, excuse me, but *is* there a connection?"

She looked at me like I'd just screwed up a long division problem at the blackboard. "Oh, Harry, who *cares* if there is! The point, you see, is that people always do assume, or think about, such things in connection with such organizations. And the surprise of Mr. Crews matters because *I* asked him the question. With you, of course, or someone like you, he would have expected it and would have given a better performance. But he thought of me as a simple, stupid nun, you see, and so he wasn't prepared for that type of question, and therefore his embarrassment when I asked it means he wished he *had* been ready for it."

She was quiet for a moment, while I stared at my desk top with Cacciatore's card still on it. *My rag is preparing a piece on charity scams—very big-buck causes that are really cover operations for some very nasty goings-on.*

The raspy voice went on. If it was anybody else, you'd call it a whiskey voice. "I don't know who Mr. Crews is connected with, Harry. But I am very sure his first loyalty isn't to E.I., and I'm very afraid E.I. itself may be mixed up with something very big and quite dangerous. And, frankly, I don't know if we have any business getting further involved."

She wasn't frightened. I knew her well enough to know that. I just couldn't quite figure out what she *was.*

"Bridget," I said. "What about Poor Fred? What about your wanting to charge into this, before we *had* a client, like a bull in a china shop?"

"I think you mean *cow,*" she corrected me. "But, at any rate, it's mainly because of 'poor Fred,' as you keep calling him, that I think we should bow out. Or not because of him, but because of his wife, his child—I don't know, Harry, call it whatever you want, intuition, superstition, insight. I have a bad feeling that we're likely to do more damage to people the further we go in this."

"Well, Bridget, in the first place I don't know where the hell we have gone in this. And when you start trying to run down a killer, people usually do get hurt. It's kind of the point, you know?"

She flushed. "No, it *isn't* the point! The point ought to be that the guilty pay and the innocent are reconciled to their sorrow. It ought to be, but I don't think it's going to turn out that way now. Look, Harry, I grant you that I wanted to find Fred's killer for revenge—for Father, for a lot of things. But vengeance isn't a simple thing. It *spreads,* more than I want it to spread. Oh, Harry, why *did* God make irreconcilable good and the means of good?"

"Uh, beg pardon?"

"Shelley. *Prometheus Unbound.*"

"Oh." I considered asking if that was Morris K. Shelley, the famous Armenian wrestler, but decided against it. She was being too serious.

"The long and short of it, dear, is that we must stop. We can return Mrs. Wright's retainer, apologize but insist that we see no way to regain the notorious package, reassure her that its location is probably safe with Fred's corpse—*anything,* Harry. As long as we stop and stop now."

"No," I said.

Now, you want to tell me that I'd been trying to keep out of the whole thing from square one, and that Bridget, and Marianne, and Fred, Jr., and even the late Fred, had been doing their damndest to drag me in. And you want to tell me that it was pure, polyunsaturated dumb of me, now that my boss finally agreed that the game was out of our class, to want to stay in. Especially, I hear you saying, since by staying in I was committing myself to keeping on the wrong side of Carp, Knobby, and whoever was probably waiting to fix my clock tonight at Northwestern.

Don't tell me. I already told myself.

"Bridget, my sweet," I went on while she stared (I think she wanted to tell me, too). "First, I don't know a damn thing about Occam or Girdle. Second, I don't know *why* God made—what was it?"

"Irreconcilable."

"Right. Irreconcilable good and the means of good. Hell, nobody even told me he *did.* And if he did, I don't care. What I do know is this. We're already *in*. Enough in that we can't get out. You've heard the phrase, 'take the King's shilling?' Well, we've taken the Wrights' shilling, and in Chicago that's about the same thing. The Wrights are *strong,* kid. And we're not going to be able to pull out until we find their bloody package, or think of a damned good reason for them to want us *not* to find it. Not after what we've already heard from them. And," I took a deep breath, thought what the hell? and went on, "speaking of things we've heard. There are a few things I'm going to tell you now, legal responsibilities or no legal responsibilities. You can either listen while I whisper them in your shell-like ear, or you can run the hell out of the room."

And then I told her.

Yup, buckaroos, I told her the whole tale. Marianne's visit, my cute little obstruction of justice, Fred's tape, the full details of my jitterbug with Knobby at Ryan's Pub, my interview with Carp (a further obstruction of justice, if you're counting), and my conversation with the Harmon of all the Wrights. I also told her about my meeting with Mr. Cacciatore, not a half-hour before she'd come into the office, and showed her the address where Cacciatore had told me to drop the envelope. Knowing Bridget and her concern to avoid violence to anybody she liked, I was sure she would tell me I couldn't possibly keep the meeting tonight, and I was ready, by God, for once to be guided by her instincts.

"Well, of course you have to keep the meeting tonight, whatever else may occur," she said. Then she looked like a cantaloupe for a minute, and sighed.

She doesn't sigh a lot, but when she does, you feel that you're a spectator at an event. She sighs the way Tug McGraw throws a baseball—you get the feeling her whole body is involved in the moment, and that the final effect (her sigh, Tug's slider) is just the conclusion of an elaborate, complicated performance.

"Yes," she exhaled at the end of the sigh. And gulped air back into her lungs. "Thank you for telling me, Harry. It clarifies a great deal, and of course it does mean that we can't withdraw now. I assume, by the way, that Fred's tape is safe?"

I assured her it was locked away with my nylon socks, patterned underwear, clip-on bow ties, and other things so ugly that even a dedicated burglar would find his gorge rising in disgust before he got to the cassette.

"Good," she nodded. "I'm afraid, though, that now everything I feared before is really about to come true."

"Aargh?"

"Oh, *you* know, Harry. Now we know at least why Fred was killed, although we still have no way of proving it. And, even if we do prove it, just think about the agony it is all bound to cause. No, dear, you were right at the beginning, we should have kept our noses out of the affair. But now," and she gave a minor sigh, a change-up, "I suppose we have to follow it all to the end, like a boring sum on the blackboard."

It was my turn to stare, and I took it. Then I asked Bridget, throwing self-respect to the winds, why Fred was killed. *She* stared.

"Well, Harry, if you really don't know, perhaps I shouldn't tell you till after your meeting tonight. It might make things safer for you."

And then I really began to worry.

• 14

SOMEDAY I'll die and, so my mom and others used to tell me, go to heaven. And there Saint Peter (after noting that I'm a Czech and weaseling an appropriate plus mark in the ledger) will ask me what I've done to deserve admission. I remember, as a kid, wondering if they stamped your hand when they let you in; you know, in case you got bored and decided to duck out for a while, like in amusement parks.

Anyhow, when he asks me the Big Question, I've got two answers ready for him that ought to get me instant entry and ten free Skeeball games.

I did not, on the night of my senior high school prom, eighty-six the presumed virginity of Martha Sue Elliot, despite the fact that she was my date, was horny-drunk out of her skull, and was draped like a *Penthouse* pet-of-the-month across the back seat of my old man's Nash Rambler stationwagon.

And I did not, on the night of my meeting with the man at the Northwestern rock, ask for any help from anybody. Not from Carp, not from my millionaire-bastard employers, not even (sort of) from Bridget O'Toole.

I know, I know. They're both negative virtues. But, like they say, you had to be there. You had to know Martha Sue Elliot in her hotpants teenage prime. And you had to know how scared I was as I walked, at nine-twenty, toward the campus.

The password, at least, wouldn't be hard to remember. It *was* as cold as a witche's tit (and I know, having met Martha Sue long after the prom, on very different terms).

I had parted from Bridget with the promise to call her as soon as my mission tonight was over. Oddly enough, she had insisted that I was probably in no danger anyhow. Not that I wanted her to worry about me, you know. But you'd think a man about to lay his hog on the table for the sake of truth, justice, and the American way deserved at least a little clucking solicitude, especially from a former professional in the clucking line. But I'd stopped trying to figure her—or anything, for that matter—out. One-foot-in-front-of-the-other Harry, that was me.

I'd spent the rest of the afternoon writing up the three boring surveillances I'd been running for weeks. It helped to keep reminding myself how much the various cuckolds and cuckoldettes were going to be soaked for the bad news. And at six, after Bridget and Brenda had gone their separate ways (Bridget striding, Brenda tacking into the wind), I'd locked the office, driven to El Tipico on Dempster—not far from where Fred had been julienned—and treated myself to a martini, a double serving of enchiladas verdes, a bottle of Carta Blanca, another bottle of Carta Blanca, and coffee. It didn't take as much time as I had hoped; I was very hungry, and I've always believed anything worth eating is worth eating fast. But I whiled away another half hour or so listening to the strolling guitar players sing "Guantanamera" eighty-seven times in succession, and ignoring the waiter who wondered, I suppose, if I was planning to ask for a cot for the night. My buddy, Patrolman Al Caceres, had introduced me to El Tipico. I don't know whether he liked the food or the chance to joke with the waiters in Spanish while I looked on stupidly. Anyhow, I thought a couple of times about just phoning old Al, to see if he'd like to come out and meet me tonight. But I was being brave.

So, at nine o'clock, I left for the rock.

The rock is in the middle of Northwestern University, and Northwestern University looks a lot like every other university I've seen on the half-time shows of Saturday football games: ugly. Lots of goofy modern buildings that haven't got the nerve to decide whether they want to be tall or spacious, so what they do is, they squat. Lots of open land full of grass and students in the summer and spring, and full of ice and mud for the other six months, serving no purpose except to keep the squatting buildings apart and screw up the tax base for everybody else who owns real estate in Evanston. Maybe it's because I didn't finish college myself; maybe it's just sour grapes envy. But I have yet to see a college campus that doesn't look more like a cleverly disguised meat-processing plant than a place people go to learn to think.

Anyhow, the rock. It's just that, a big rock sitting right in front of University Hall, which is the only really distinctive building on the campus since it was built a hundred years ago, in imitation of the Chicago Water Tower, and so is ugly at least in a different way from the playpen Bauhaus spreading out around it. Students, so runs the tradition, regularly paint the rock different colors and scrawl various suggestive, subversive, or just silly slogans across it. Some fun. I guess even the most dedicated citizen of tomorrow needs a break from frisbee, grass, and rock-and-roll once in a while.

It took me fifteen minutes to drive from El Tipico east to the Northwestern campus, and another five or ten to find a parking place among the ridges of snow the plows had left along the curbs. I was only a block or so from the rock.

Funny thing, but I've always noticed how those great, heavy-weight moral choices you make during the day start to look like damn silly mistakes when it comes time to pay up on them. It's like the vasectomy I had a few years ago. The pill was dangerous, right; a man should share the responsibility for birth control, right; seemed like the most reasonable thing in the world. And then came the morning of the operation itself, with me in a pre-op gown, about to serve up my prize possessions to novocaine and the knife. I just could *not* remember why this had all once seemed so sensible.

Then and now, I felt like a harp seal who couldn't wait to be clubbed by an enterprising Canadian, and so bashed his own skull against the nearest rock just for the hell of it.

And the rock was what I was walking toward. The National Weather Service, according to my car radio, said that the temperature was five degrees above zero with a windchill of minus fifteen. That meant it was a clear night. And *that* meant my contact, standing out by the rock in tail-freezing weather and full moonlight, would be about as inconspicuous as a nose wart.

And there he was, whoever the hell he was. A guy bundled up in a scarf, an overcoat, and a big Russian-style fur cap. Not as big as Cacciatore, but still a lot bigger than I could imagine myself being. He looked familiar, somehow.

I sauntered up, we exchanged the passwords set by whatever spy movie freak was arranging this thing, and then got down to business.

As I handed him the pack of cigarettes, as per my instructions, he grabbed my right wrist. And I mean *grabbed* it—if I wanted to try and twist free, the force of the grab told me I'd have to face a lot more trouble than that.

"Listen," he husked at me. "Are you sure there's nobody with you?" Clouds of steam billowed from behind his scarf.

There wasn't, I husked back. It was like sending messages through smoke signals.

"Good. Then come with me." And then he did something amazing, something I've only seen done two or three times before. He let go my wrist and just strolled off. Two kinds of guys will do that: fools, and guys so sure of themselves that they *know*, if you know what's good for you, you'll follow. Guys, in other words, trying to impress you.

I was impressed. I followed him.

We walked to his car, an old Volkswagen Beetle, got in, and began driving west onto Clark Street. My host was still muffled up like the Lone Ranger and—call me impulsive—I'd been kidnapped enough lately that I was losing patience.

"Look," I said, "whoever you are. Can you explain why the hell we have to go through all this? Did I accidentally run over your dog, or what?" I didn't really expect a decent answer, of course. And once again life proved its constant ability to disappoint us.

The driver pulled off his cap, unwrapped his scarf, and turned a grin on me. "Mr. Garnish, I'd be glad to explain," he said. "My name is Ed Brady—we've met before, actually—and I work for, well, really, I *run*, Northshore Investigations Agency."

Of course he was, and of course he did. I'd seen him a couple of times at North Chicago private eye dinners, where he was sometimes guest speaker, and I'd seen him once or twice walking through the halls of Northshore when I'd gone to pick up Fred for a drink after work. Ed Brady had paid his dues as a Chicago cop, and then for some years as a working member of the private snitch infantry, but that was all long before my time. Now he lived in an expensive North Shore home—probably not far from

Harmon Wright's shack—kept the shit off his shoes, and, only when he felt like it, checked in on the agency he had built up into one of the best and most profitable in town. For my line of work, he was the success story I'd kept telling myself would be mine some day.

Kidnapped or not, I was traveling in some fast company these days.

"Hello," I said.

"Hello," he said. "By the way, what name did the fellow who contacted you this afternoon use?"

"Cacciatore."

"Oh, no. *Really?*" he laughed. "We're going to have to talk to him about his cover names. He's a new man in the area, and I think he's trying to show off a little. Would you believe a month ago he had a passport and driver's license forged in the name of Jack Salmon?"

"Swell," I said. "Repossess his cookbooks or put him on a diet. Is that why I'm being hassled, because I eat a TV dinner once in a while?"

Brady laughed again, like he thought I was the funniest thing he'd seen since *Earthquake*. "Harry, believe me, if you want me to stop and let you off somewhere, anywhere, just say so. You're under no duress—though I take it you've had your share of duress over the last few days. Of course, you'll probably lose in the bargain, but then that's not my problem, is it? All I want to do is drive around for a while and ask you some questions. Okay?"

"Wait a minute," I said. "You mean there's no national magazine piece on charity scams? No sworn statement in an envelope you're supposed to give me to deliver? Imagine my astonishment."

Ed Brady laughed for the third time. I had the feeling he was a man who laughed a lot—not because he found many things funny, but because he thought he needed the practice. He didn't take his eyes from the road, but he did fish in his pocket and take out a cigar the size of a dirty joke, which he offered me. I took it.

"Harry, I'll be frank. This whole meeting, silly as it may look, was my idea. I could have called you at the office, I could have come to your apartment. But I needed to know a couple of things about you, before I made my—proposition—to you. I needed to know if you kept your word. You do. You came tonight without a backup. I needed to know if you were willing to take risks. You are. You agreed to the meeting in the first place. And I needed to know if you still hated your boss. And you do—you didn't tell her about this meeting, did you?"

"No," I lied.

"I thought not. You know what they say about you?"

I didn't even know who they were, except that if they had to talk about me, they must lead some pretty uninteresting lives. I told him so.

"Oh, no, Harry. You're an interesting man, even if you don't think you are. What they say—other people in the private intelligence business—is that you're a very good, very smart investigator, and that it's a goddamn shame you're stuck working for a two-bit agency like O'Toole's." The way he said "O'Toole's" he made it sound like a grocery store. "They say," he continued, "if you'd gotten a few breaks, or if you'd made a few breaks, you'd be pulling down some very big bucks by now, and not running down divorce cases for *bupkis*. But, Harry, that's only what *they* say. What do *you* say?"

"I say you either want to marry me or hire me," I said. "But, bullshit aside, I still don't know *why*."

"Oh, yes, you do," Brady said, and as he said it, slammed the VW toward the icy curb, rammed the stick into reverse at just the right moment to avoid stripping the gears, and floated like a feather into a parking space I wouldn't have tried to fill with a ten-speed bicycle. No doubt about it, the man got a kick out of being in control of things.

I hadn't been watching where we were going. It just looked like an aimless ramble around downtown Evanston, a perfect place for a secret meeting. You could taxi around in a flying saucer there on a wintry Tuesday night and feel pretty safe from interruption. But sonofagun if we weren't right in front of the Carlson Building on Church Street, the eighth floor of which housed Northshore Investigations, Incorporated.

"Come on in for a minute, Harry," Brady said, getting out of the car. "I want to show you something."

I followed him through a side entrance and a service elevator, both operated by a private key he had in his case, to the eighth floor.

Northshore Agency, as I think I've said, is a big concern. They had a whole suite of offices in the Carlson Building, and as we walked toward their front door I noticed that there were lights inside. Good old Ed Brady must have had very little doubt that I would come up with him.

In fact, he must have been lead pipe-cinch-sure that I would come with him. Because there was a reception committee waiting for me in the front office. Over by the copy machine, thumbing through *Hustler,* stood the man who called himself Cacciatore. And sitting behind the receptionist's desk, looking scared and fidgeting with a coffee cup, sat Marianne, the wounded widow of my dreams. She glanced up quickly as I walked into the office, and then began to concentrate her attention on her fingernails.

Nobody started speaking, so I assumed it was my turn. "You said I'd never see you again," I said to the man who called himself Cacciatore. "Indian giver."

He grimaced at me and turned to his boss, right behind me. "Mr. Brady, okay if I go now?"

"Sure, Pete," said Brady. "And thanks for keeping Mrs. Healey company." Pete—I wondered what his last name was, really—wrapped himself in his fuzzy coat and left by the front door without even a nod to me.

I looked at Brady. "Well?" I said.

The man who enjoyed driving like a test pilot was also enjoying watching me and Marianne avoid one another's eyes.

"Well," he said, settling down comfortably on a sofa. "I don't think we all need be so formal, do you? Come on, Harry, come on, Marianne. Why act so embarrassed? You two didn't hurt anybody, and you've got nothing to be sorry for. Right?"

It was the kind of cheerfulness that has only one purpose, to make everybody else in the room feel miserable. Marianne still didn't speak, but I saw her wince.

"Okay, Mr. Brady," I said. "We've waltzed enough, don't you think? I assume Marianne is here voluntarily, just like I am. But if you don't get to the point pretty soon, I'm going to voluntarily tell you to piss off, and the lady and I are leaving."

Brady smiled patiently. "No, you're not. Because you've already come this far, and because you must know that the lady is part of the reason I got on to you in the first place. But, all right, I will get to the point. The point is that it was me who called Marianne the night Fred was killed. The point is that you're going to solve Fred's murder—don't worry, I'm going to help you. And finally, the point is that while you solve the murder, you and I are going to make more money than I'll bet you can imagine."

I've got to give him that: He knew how to get to a point.

• 15

"I CALLED her," Brady went on, "because I was worried that Fred was getting involved in something that could be dangerous for him, and damaging for the agency."

"In that order, of course," I said. Marianne continued to stare at her hands.

Brady just sighed. Cheap shots couldn't reach him.

"Harry," he said. "I could show you the files on Healey's work for E.I. We got duplicates of everything he sent them, of course. But you'd just find them boring. You know the drill—nothing to report but a few leads are developing, nothing to report but an interesting pattern may be emerging, stuff like that."

I knew the drill, all right. I'd written the same kind of report at least a thousand times. Translated, they all read the same: I haven't found out a damned thing, but keep paying me my per diem.

"Stuff like that," Brady said, "until about a month ago." I kept my eyes on Brady's tie, where I'd been gazing since he began to talk. It always looks like your hanging on their every word, but it relieves you of worrying about signalling anything you don't want to signal with your eyes. "About a month ago" was when Yolanda Wright had said the fatal packet of cocaine was discovered by our Fred. But I didn't know that. At least not as far as the director of Northshore Investigative Agency was concerned.

"A month ago, Fred's reports changed—very briefly, but they changed. I won't bother to read them to you, as I said. But a kind of excitement began to creep into his prose, a kind of anticipation. Do you ever think about prose style, Harry—as a form of information, I mean?"

"Can't say that I have," I said.

"Well, I have," he gloated. "Think about it: one flurry of interest and excitement in that desert of boring reports, and then—suddenly—the reports become boring again. But more boring than before, Harry. Almost as if, now, they were *trying* to be boring. Why that one oasis, I thought to myself? Well, what would *you* think?"

"Uh, that Fred was hiding something?" I murmured it with my best stupid expression, and my eyes still fixed on the knot of his tie.

"Oh, baby, don't play stupid with me. Yes, Fred was hiding something. Hiding it from us—and we were still signing his checks, right? You see, part of my job is to make sure none of my operatives begins to play games like that. It can lead to blackmail, and to all sorts of other unpleasant occurrences. It's why I've learned to read reports so carefully."

Marianne had been silent all along. She spoke now in barely more than a whisper, but it came out like a shout.

"Brady, you *bastard!* I told you—I *told* you—if you think Fred was mixed up in something like that, something crooked, you never *knew* him! Harry—tell him what Fred was like!"

But since I didn't really think I was the right guy for a testimonial, I just crossed to Marianne, took her hand, and stroked her hair. It had always calmed her before, and it did now.

Brady, anyhow, was still being man of the hour, and enjoying every minute of it. "Now, now, Marianne, I'm not accusing Fred of, well, of *cheating* on me." We both stared at him, not looking at one another. It was a clever hook, and I wanted to break his nose for it. He must have gone to sonofabitch school. "No, all I mean is that I *did* notice something strange about his work. Now, maybe he was just keeping the information to himself till he had something really dramatic to show us. I don't know. But I did know enough to start checking Fred's movements a little more carefully these last few weeks, really, not out of distrust as much as out of concern. He could have been coasting for real trouble."

It struck me that in fact Fred had coasted into some real trouble—about the realest trouble you can imagine.

"Tell me, Ed," I broke in. "If I come to work for you, do I get the free nursemaid service, too?"

He didn't take any notice. "And there were a lot of irregularities in his movements over the last month. You know, Marianne, that he was out nights a great deal more than usual. And his logs were getting vaguer and vaguer.

"Well, to make a long story short, by early last week I was sure that, whatever Fred was doing, it was losing money for North-shore. And that, Harry, I do not like."

I'll bet he didn't. And I'll bet he could take it really personally. "So what about Thursday night?" I asked. "You've got your own damn detective agency, you've got your own army of snitches, and cameras, and tapes, and God knows what else. So you have to call the poor bastard's wife to find out where he is, and what he might be doing?"

Ed Brady shook his head, and looked really—I mean really—disappointed in me, like I had just failed a test designed for my own poor abilities. Why, I wondered, did everybody get such a charge out of treating me like the class dunce.

"Harry. No. Obviously I didn't need to know where he would be that night. And obviously, also, the Skokie CTA lot is a smart place for a meeting. In an open area like that, late at night, a smart agent could spot a tail with one eye shut. And Fred was a smart agent. Besides, I didn't want to find out exactly what he was into—at least not yet. You know, Harry—the magic half hour?"

I knew. It's a formula everybody in the business hears their first week on the job, and only learns after a year or so *on* the job. We all want to get our information as soon as possible. Clients want it, snoopers want it, just plain human beings want it. If there's something I should know, let me know it and let me know it *right now*. But things don't work that way.

More surveillances have been blown because of overeager investigators than for any other reason. So, the magic half hour. You trail your couple to the motel, you watch them get the key and go into the room, you make sure your camera is loaded and that the flash battery is fully charged, and then you go around the corner and have a cup of coffee for *exactly* one half hour. Less than that and you're liable to bust open the door and get a candid shot of two fully clothed people sharing a drink. Big fat hairy deal. Much longer than that and you're liable to get a shot of a guy zipping up his pants. Ditto. So you wait. And then, bingo! you've got just what you need. But the waiting is hard to learn. Ed Brady was obviously damned good at it.

"No," he droned on. "I called Marianne that night because I wanted to know two or three things about *her*. I wanted to know if *she* knew where Fred was going to be, and she did. That meant she might know more than just where he was. She might know what the whole scene was about, might even be able to point me toward whatever gold mine Fred had stumbled on. And, more important, I wanted to know if she was loyal. I was counting on her not being, of course."

I glanced quickly at her, half expecting her to rise to leave, or to blow up again. But she didn't, and I knew why. She had heard this calm, droning voice say all these ugly things about her before. It was part of why she was here. She expected it.

"You know, Harry, you and Marianne have been a gossip item so long that nobody even bothers to joke about you any more. No offense, but that's the way it is. And I was hoping that she would be—well, alienated—enough from Fred by now to blow his cover to me. She didn't know who I was, of course. I could have been a friend of Fred's, or a real danger to him. So, if she told me where he was, it meant she could be reached, later, about other things. I was pretty proud of myself, actually; it was a nice little bit of psychology." And he smiled for the first time like he really meant it.

"Right," I said. "Wonderful psychology, Ed. Good for you. Marianne, come on. We're leaving." I took her hand and she rose. I don't think she really cared what the hell she did. And then Brady did what I'd been hoping he would do since we had come into the office. He broke control.

He moved quickly to the door and stood before it like a linebacker. His face lost its shit-eating grin. "Not yet, Harry," he rasped. "Not till you've heard the rest."

So he *didn't* hold all the cards. There was something—damned if I could guess what it was—he needed, or needed to know, from me. Good. When you've spent your life, like I have, trying to keep out of the way of wolves, you learn to look for tiny handles that might be used, in a pinch, as bludgeons.

"Okay," I said, keeping hold of Marianne's hand. "What's the rest?"

He relaxed a little. "The rest, of course, is that I had no way of knowing Fred was going to be killed that night. That's *true,* Harry. But, since he was killed, it gave me—sorry, my dear— another bit of leverage."

"Jesus, Brady," I said, and the awe in my voice was real, "you really do think that way, don't you?"

I think he thought it was a compliment. "Harry, *think*! As soon as I heard, Friday morning, about Fred's death, I knew I'd have to talk to the police. And in Skokie, that means Inspector Carp. Now, Clarence Carp and I are old friends. You didn't know that, did you?"

I didn't, but I was beginning to understand how logical it would be.

"Oh, yes," he went on. "I've done Lance"—Lance?" a few odd favors, over the years, and he's always returned them. A private detective doesn't *have* to be treated like a dog turd by the officials, you know. That's just Hollywood, an it's damned bad for business, too. All it takes is a little, well, a little accommodation here and there, and life becomes much simpler. So, anyhow, I knew Lance Carp would be talking not only to me but to the widow, here. And I was sure, too, I could trust him to tell me whether the widow mentioned anything about an anonymous phone call the night of the murder. Oh, not that he would foul up a murder investigation just to please me. But if I give my word to Lance that something is a strictly private matter—just business, you know—he usually takes it. You know?"

I didn't know that one, either, but I could imagine. Ninety percent, and I'm being conservative, of the homicides the police department solves are solved not by a careful piecing together of clues but by information gained from informers. So if you're a *professional* informer, and if the cops know you're good for lots and lots of information in the vague future, it's only logical that once in a while they'll cut the cards your way—let you in on something you need to know from them, no questions asked. Especially if you call the chief inspector of the homicide division "Lance."

"And do you know what?" Ed Brady said triumphantly. "Marianne here didn't breathe a word about my call, not in three separate interviews with the police. Not even after she was shot!

That meant she had to be afraid of something. So I went to see her Sunday night after she got out of the hospital, and"—he smiled at her, the bastard—"that's when she told me about telling *you*. What she was afraid of, at least after she was shot, was that somebody might find out *you* knew about the call!"

Terrific. I'd obstructed justice, put my butt in a sling, for nothing. But I didn't have time to get bitter over that now. "Listen," I said. "When you found out Marianne hadn't mentioned the call to Carp—when you found out she'd told me about the call—did you tell Carp?"

He spread his hands. "Well, Harry. What *could* I do? What I did, actually, was just let Carp know—Sunday night it was—that it might be worth his while to sound you out." Swell. That explained better than Carp had why the Skokie P.D. hadn't seen fit to hassle me until three days after Fred bought his farm. "Of course," continued Ed Brady, "I didn't let him know any of the more complicated bits of the situation. They weren't really his business, anyhow. And I'm sure they wouldn't help lead him to Fred's killer. Aren't you?"

Wasn't I what? *What* "more complicated bits of the situation?" I was about to ask him that when Marianne did two funny things. She dropped my hand, and she grabbed the coffee cup in front of her and threw it, violently, to the floor. It was plastic, naturally, so it didn't shatter; just bounced, like a frightened mole, off toward the nearest corner of the room. And then she shouted.

"Goddammit, Brady, *tell* him!" was what she shouted.

"Yes, of course, Marianne. I was coming to that." Ed Brady was back to enjoying himself. Which meant that, whatever it was he had to tell me, I wasn't going to enjoy it: that much at least I had learned about the man. I didn't look at Marianne.

"What our friend wants me to tell you, Harry, is that when I saw her on Sunday night, she told me a little more than about your phone call intrigue. She confessed to me that the reason she went to you in the first place was that she thought she would need some protection—and protection from somebody who understood our business. That was before she had spoken to me, of course." I made a mental note that Ed Brady said "of course" a lot—a sure sign that a guy is a self-satisfied prick. It's what he would call prose style as a means of information.

"Now," he went on, "she understands that you both need my protection."

"At no extra charge?" I tried to snarl. I've never been able to work myself up to a real snarl, but I came pretty close this time.

But my host was still unfazed. "Well, anyhow," he shook himself back to the business at hand. "Marianne told me that she had been receiving money for some time now in the mail. Not checks, mind you—cash money. A hundred dollars, in twenties, every week for the last six weeks; delivered every Tuesday in an envelope with her name on it and no return address. And only the first letter had a message in it. What did it say, Marianne?"

"It said," Marianne said, " 'More to come. You'll find out why when it's time.' " She glared at Brady. "Wouldn't *you* keep it? You self-satisfied bastard, wouldn't *you* keep it?"

"Hey," I said. "It's okay. Nobody's hitting on you, Marianne—are we, Ed?" She was on the edge of something, and I didn't want to see her fall off of it, even though I felt like an Olympic-class sucker. Why hadn't she told *me* about the money?

"Thank you, Harry," said Brady. "The point is, Marianne didn't know what kind of investigation, or what kind of intrigue her husband was involved in. But she had been getting money— quite a bit of money—and had been wise enough to keep quiet about it. And she cared little enough about her husband to indicate, to me, his location on the night he was killed. Now, what does that all add up to?"

He paused and glanced at us both. Maybe he was expecting one of us to raise a hand. We didn't. He sighed.

"What it adds up to is this, of course. Whether she knows it or not, Marianne has been in the employ of someone since she received, and kept, that first envelope. And the someone, I'm sure we can all guess, is also someone connected with Fred's death. Just as my anonymous phone call was a test of her loyalty to her husband, this was a test, too, although a test by person or persons with considerably more resources than I possess. Fair enough?"

It was fair enough. He may have been a sonofabitch, but he was a smart sonofabitch.

"Now," he continued, "I don't know what's in the stew Fred cooked, and I don't particularly want to know what's in the stew

Fred cooked. But I know that there was a stew, and that it's still there, and that somewhere along the line Harmon Wright, and Ecology International, and a *lot* of money is involved."

How many people could you work for on a single case? I wondered. Mrs. Wright and Mr. Wright had already paid me money, and now it looked like Brady was about to get out his checkbook, too. People sure were happy to pay me these days— especially considering I didn't know what, exactly, they were paying me to do.

Brady went on. "Now, E.I. obviously wants things kept nice, quiet, and normal. And nice and normal is the way we're going to keep them, Harry. We found out today—never mind how—that you're now the agent of record for E.I. Or, rather, that O'Toole Agency is. I couldn't be happier. Mrs. Wright is some persuasive lady, huh?"

Marianne looked at me. I didn't say a thing.

"Right. Well," he went on, "I can give you Fred's killer on a silver plate, garnished, with asparagus. And I can give him to you so that nobody at Ecology International gets any shit on their shoes."

I couldn't help myself, I gulped. "Who was it?"

Brady licked his chops. "Well, you know, it wasn't *anybody,* really. If you know what I mean. It was obviously a mechanic, a pro, and Christ knows where he's gotten to by now."

"Won't wash," I said. "Mechanics don't mess with people the way they messed with Fred, and you know it."

"Ah, there you're wrong. See, a pro who really wanted the job to look amateur *would* pull something like that. It's a clever way to cover up a paid job as looking like the work of a lunatic."

I could only stare. Even if he *didn't* believe any of that crap, it was beautiful. Just like Ed Brady to pick the most outrageous lie he could and then assert it like he was saying, "It's snowing outside."

"The way I see it, Fred must've found out some kind of underworld connection at Ecology International. Probably nothing serious, the Wrights are squeaky clean, but some minor fucker dabbling in something he shouldn't be dabbling in. Okay, let's say Fred tries to follow the thing up, and maybe stumbles on to a mob connection that's still alive. Bad news for the connection, bad news for the Wrights, bad news all around. So the connection has Fred offed. Sorry, Marianne."

He was a man with beautiful manners.

"Okay," I said. "I'm slow-witted, so let me get this lined up. You want me to find out that Fred was killed by a phantom who's since then moved to Cleveland, right? And you want me to tell the cops that it's all because of a Mafia connection with E.I., but that they shouldn't worry their heads about it because it's such a *tiny* Mafia connection, right? And they're going to believe me because nobody wants to see the wonderful Wrights dirtied by any of this. And for this you drag me up here at," I looked at my watch, "eleven at night. Are you *crazy?*"

"No, I'm not. I guarantee it will work. Look. The mob connection lets the police off the hook, because any investigation of a mob connection with E.I. can now be carried on with the cooperation of the Wrights. It makes them look like the good citizens they are, instead of like people who may have been concealing something. Okay? And if the connection is found, fine and good. And if it isn't, the investigation itself keeps all parties looking nice. And, since Northshore is comfortably out of things, I can go with a clear conscience to . . . certain people—and get a healthy emolument for arranging things so efficiently."

"You mean," I said, "get juice from the Wrights for doing their public relations work, or for having me do their public relations work." Something was very wrong with all of this, and I couldn't quite figure out what. Oh, not that it was a convenient lie to get us all out of the woods; that didn't scare me especially. But the more Brady talked, the more I began to realize that it was a lie that could be—scarily—close to the truth. He didn't know, I assumed, about the packet of cocaine Yolanda Wright wanted me to find. And he sure as hell didn't know about Fred's tape, still safe back in my desk. But everything in the lie he'd invented made sense out of what the richest woman in Chicago and the dead man had told me, not to mention what I'd seen of the wild-eyed innocence of the richest man and most dedicated whale saver in town. So what was wrong with it—I mean, why did it give me a creepy feeling, the way you feel when you're dreaming a dream you *know* is a dream, but still can't control what happens in the dream? I wished Bridget and her friend Girdle were there to explain it.

"Believe me, Harry, the story not only makes sense, it turns a disaster for some very important people—very important people, Harry—into a plus sign. I've already talked this out with Marianne, and she agrees that it's the best thing to do."

I looked at Marianne, who'd found something fascinating about her fingernails again. "And who shot *you?*" I said to her. "Do you think a cockeyed story like this is going to keep you protected?"

"Nothing to protect her from," crooned Brady. "Her shooting obviously had nothing to do with Fred's death. Just some local idiot trying out his new mail-order gun; it does happen all the time, you know."

"Dammit, Brady . . ." I began, but he raised his hand.

"And, face it, Harry, if you want Marianne to be safe—even if our little explanation doesn't explain everything—don't you think that any explanation that puts the whole thing to rest, you know, takes pressure off certain people, that *any* explanation like that could be her best insurance policy?"

Once again, it sounded almost true. "Is your mother watching Fred, Jr.?" I asked Marianne. I couldn't ask her what I wanted to: if she was really willing to sweep Fred under the carpet for some bread and the feeling of being safe.

"Oh—oh, no," said Marianne. "My mother flew back to California this morning. Fred is spending the night at Mrs. Girard's." I had a feeling Mrs. Girard was going to get a lot of chances to work off her maternal instincts.

"Right," I said to Brady. "I'll give you my answer tomorrow."

"I know you will," he said. "You'll give it to me by ten o'clock tomorrow morning. At this number." He flipped a card to me. "And if the answer is no, I'm sure I don't have to tell you how quiet to keep about our little conversation. Of course, if you say no, we'll just have to arrange the whole thing through another route of information to the police, so there's no point in your cutting yourself out, is there, Harry? Well, you think about it hard. And now I'll take you back to your car. Oh, would you do me a favor and see Mrs. Healey home?"

Marianne and I didn't talk very much as I drove to her house. I was mad as hell. As far as I could tell, her visit to me after Fred's death had been more a test than a confession. Would I help her lie to the cops? Sure thing, just tell old H. Garnish what law you want broken, blow in his ear, and watch him go to work. Anything else I can do—move the corpse around before the coroner's photographer arrives? Right on. Just tell me what position you'd like him in. Ed Brady, at least, loved playing head games like that with people, and Marianne had been seeing more of Ed Brady than I liked, and I didn't even know that she hadn't been seeing more of him than I knew.

Not that I said any of this. She looked miserable enough without the benefit of my scathing wit. But if I opened my mouth at all, I knew I'd start in. So I kept my mouth shut. It's not the best way to communicate. We drove the six miles to her house in noisy silence, carefully not saying all the things we had to say to one another. It was almost like being married.

I skidded into a space near her house. "You have to pick up Fred, Jr.?" I said to the windshield.

"No. I told you, he's staying the night. Mrs. Girard said she'd give him breakfast. She likes to play with him in the mornings."

"Mrs. Girard's a nice lady."

"Harry." She put her hand on my knee. "I'm sorry. I thought it would all be better for me and for you, too. Fred *is* dead."

I watched it start snowing again. "Yeah, he sure the hell is that. Look, kid, don't worry—everybody makes choices, which means everybody makes mistakes."

She grasped my knee a little harder. "Won't you—couldn't you—come in?"

I looked at her. She'd been shot up, had been dragged to a seedy private eye's office with not enough rest, her long brown hair looked like it hadn't been brushed in a week, and she was dressed more for a volleyball game than a seduction. But the streetlight caught half her face and both her eyes, and her eyes were very soft and very serious.

"Really, Harry, it's all *right*. Come on in, huh?"

What the hell. It had been a long time, and I could call Bridget O'Toole tomorrow. I went in.

• 16

WEDNESDAY morning I woke up at eight o'clock to the sounds and smells of coffee perking and bacon frying. It felt so damned good, and so damned *corny,* that I just lay there for a few minutes enjoying it all. If this was the payoff, I thought, maybe Ed Brady's proposition of the night before was worth taking seriously.

I pulled on my pants and flip-flopped into the kitchen. There was Marianne, looking like the daydream of an especially horny Dagwood Bumstead and fiddling with a fork over a skillet. Her hair is dark and long, and at this hour of the morning it wasn't as frazzled as the night before, but it also wasn't brushed or pinned or any other such nonsense. Why do women, I wonder, think that their hair looks better when it's organized? Do you enjoy *planned* outings? And she was wearing nothing but a purple house-coat that might have come off the rack at K-Mart, but that gathered around her butt in a way that would have made a sculptor weep.

I know, I know. I believe in the ERA, and I believe that women are people, too. It's just that sometimes I backslide.

"Hi," she smiled at me, turning, but still stirring the bacon. "Why don't you get us both a cup of coffee?" I kissed her lightly. Corny, corny, corny. I loved it.

I got us both a cup of coffee. We had the kind of breakfast everybody ought to have all the time: happy, with lots of chatter about nothing at all and lots of private smiles about the night before. Bacon and eggs and the brass ring. It was all so nice that I almost forgot about having to ruin it all. But not quite.

With my third cup of coffee I ran back to the bedroom to fetch my cigarettes from my jacket. I put my shirt back on, lit up, and pulled on last night's socks and my shoes. Then, feeling less vulnerable, I strolled back into the kitchen, where she was still sitting with a heartmelting smile on her face.

"Listen," I said, swallowing coffee on top of smoke, and leaning against the door. "We've got to talk, and we've got to talk seriously."

The smile fell. "You really want out, don't you?" she said. "I mean out of all this," and she glared around the kitchen as if Ed Brady, the Wrights, and Inspector Carp were perched on the toaster and peeking out from the garbage disposal.

"Kid," I sighed, "I don't even know what *this* is, if you want the truth. But Brady's going to be expecting a call from me, and Mr. Harmon Wright is going to be checking in with me, and Mrs. Yolanda Wright is going to want a report, and even my boss, you know, might like to hear a little something from me before spring. And, dammit, I don't know what to tell all those people. Because I don't know where you and I stand, for Christ's sake, in all *this*. Like, for instance, why didn't you tell me about the cash you were getting in the mail? And why didn't you call me after Brady contacted you? Dammit, Marianne—do you have any idea how fucking *scared* I was last night when I went to keep that appointment?"

I was getting angrier than I'd meant to get. But that was all right, because I was also getting more involved than I'd wanted to be. Some time between last night and my second cup of coffee at breakfast, I'd discovered a funny thing. I was really in love with Marianne, and I cared a hell of a lot what happened to her, and to us. Maybe that's what I was really angry about.

She looked about as miserable as I was starting to feel.

"Oh, Harry," she said. "I couldn't tell you about Ed Brady, or about the money. I was scared too, damn it! I was scared that if I told you about the money you'd think I was—was—involved in Fred's death, and then I would lose you, too! And, Harry, I *love* you, and it isn't enough . . ." she shook her head and began to cry.

Well, it wasn't enough I suppose. It sure the hell wouldn't have satisfied Perry Mason. But then I wasn't a cross-examiner, and besides, Perry Mason hadn't spent the night in bed with Marianne. I put down my cup, dropped my cigarette in it, crossed to her, and hugged her. Just hugged her.

"Kid. It's enough. Believe me, it's enough. I mean, anybody silly enough to love me is probably too damn silly to act sensible anyhow, am I right?" She gave a half-moan, half-laugh. "Look," I went on. "You go and get dressed, okay? Then we'll try to sort this all out and decide what we ought to do. But don't worry— dig? Whatever happens, you're not going to get burned. I'll make sure of that. And you're not going to lose, kid. I'll make double sure of that."

She smiled one of those glistening eye smiles that most guys I know would impale themselves on a rusty spike for, and went off to get dressed while I poured myself another cup of coffee.

That fourth cup of coffee in the morning is a bastard. It's what puts the edge on your day, starts you thinking all the smart, cagey things you know you're supposed to be thinking. But it's also what puts you *over* another kind of edge, the adrenalin edge, maybe. You not only start thinking all the smart things, but you're pissed off about the smart things you're thinking. By the time Marianne, still smiling, came back, dressed in a mouse-brown suit, it was nine-thirty and I had decided (a) I was behaving like an adolescent donkey, (b) last night, for all the groaning and hollering, was probably just one more carrot dangled in front of the adolescent donkey I was acting like, and (c) Fred Healey hadn't been dead for a week, and already his wife was screwing around again, and nobody seemed to give a healthy damn. Except me.

"Well, my genius," chirped Marianne as she draped her arms around me. "Any ideas?"

I shrugged her off and walked over to pour cup number five. "Some," I said. "But none of them very nice. The way I see it," I said, sipping nonchalantly with my hand shaking, "is this. Fred was iced for a reason nobody cares a hell of a lot about. Okay? Okay. And you and Ed Brady—sorry, Ed Brady, with you following his lead—want to cap the whole thing as quick as possible and maybe make some heavy bread out of it all, since Fred, or you, or Ed, was lucky enough to be working for some very rich folks when his doorbell got rung. Am I right so far?"

From her look, I might as well have thrown the coffee pot at her head. Not that I could blame her. You try leaving a lover to walk into the other room, and coming back to find the Spanish Inquisition waiting for you.

I went on. "So, since I'm obviously the pivot of the whole

operation, and since nobody around seems to give a rat's ass about why Fred might have really got killed, I figure we might as well go along with the scheme. Even though it's a pretty slimy scheme, you know, Marianne?"

"Oh, Harry, what is it?" she almost wailed. "Why are you saying these things?"

"Well, for two reasons. Because they're true. They are the bottom line, you know? And because, if the shit really hits the fan in all of this, Inspector Clarence Carp of the Skokie P.D. is going to say the same things to you, but a lot harder. Okay?"

"Okay," she sighed. Maybe the coffee was wearing off, or maybe I'm just not the bully I like to think I am. For whatever reason, I was feeling stupid about my sermon.

"No need to thank me," I said. "Now we're going to cover as many bases as we can. I'm going to call Ed Brady now, and I'm going to tell him that our little deal is on. He can feed me the information he wants to feed me, he can point me towards the cops he wants to spring the information on, whatever."

Her face began to relax into a smile, but I went on.

"And then," I said, "after I call Brady, I'm calling Harmon Wright and I'm letting him know that I've got on to something. I'm letting him know that I've got enough information to make him and his damned save-the-whale foundation look good, and I'm asking him what he wants me to do with it. But that's not all. Then I'm calling Carp, I'm letting *him* know that I'm officially working for Wright on this thing, and I'm telling him that he and Ed Brady are a couple of bastards in collusion. He already knows both those facts, but I think it'll be worth our while to remind him that they're not state secrets."

Her eyes were wide enough by now that I shut up. "Harry," she said, "are you sure this is how you want to work things?"

"No," I said. "But I'm sure that I don't want Ed Brady telling me how to work things, and I'm sure that the more information I spread around, the more people will have a vested interest in keeping me around to spread more information. And the safer you and I will be. We're playing pretty fast and loose with murder as it is, you know?"

"All right, darling," she said. And walked over to me and kissed me. This time I didn't shrug her off.

For a plan improvised in ten minutes after a night of frantic screwing, I think it wasn't half-bad. Unfortunately, I never got the chance to find out how it would have worked.

Marianne kept her arms around me all the way to the wall phone. I fished in my pockets for the number Brady had given me, found it, and dialled it. A soft, Southern-sounding voice answered.

"Unh—Hello, Brady residence."

"Unh—yes, ma'am. Hello. May I speak to Mr. Brady, please?"

"*Mister* Brady?" There was an odd undercurrent of concern in her voice, whoever she was.

"Yes, ma'am. Mister Brady. Tell him it's the call he was expecting at ten this morning."

"Unh, yes. Could you wait a moment, please?" I listened to that familiar sound of feet tick-tacking away from the receiver at the other end; muffled conversation; and heavier feet clack-clacking back to the phone.

I hung up.

I also went stiff all over, and my forehead started to sweat, you know, like in a gin hangover. The quiet, courteous voice on the other end of the wire wasn't Ed Brady. It was, and no mistake about it if you'd heard it once, the voice of Clarence Carp, the terror of criminals in Skokie and "Lance" to his very few friends.

Something was wrong. Was I being set up, I wondered, for another of Brady's damned psychological tests?

"Harry, what . . ." began Marianne.

"*Quiet!*" I shouted. She got all rigid, too, while I dialled the number of Northshore Detective Agency. Thank God, I thought, I hadn't given my name to the maid at Ed Brady's. See, some of the things they taught you about good manners are wrong. A secretary answered in the bored voice of a computer tape.

"Northshore Agency, good morning," she said.

"Good mornin'," I said in my best booming voice. "Say, ma'am, I wonder if you could put me in touch with Mr.—unh, hold on here a minute—oh, *yeah*, Mr. Edward Brady? Tell 'im this is Bob Hielscher from Magnum Advertisin' callin', okay? We want to talk to Mr. Brady about doin' some security work for us down here."

The computer voice began to melt into something human. But it was anxiety that was doing the melting.

"Mr. Hielscher, is it? Sir, may I ask where, where you are calling from?"

"Why, *hell,* honey, I'm callin' from Magnum Advertisin's offices, don't you know." Marianne was staring at me like I'd lost my mind. But—smart girl—she didn't make a sound while I was doing my Bob Hielscher Act. "Now, you listen here," I went on before the anonymous secretary could hang up or switch me to a pre-tapped line, "do I get to talk to Mr. Brady, or do I got to call some other agency? This is *business,* darlin'!"

"Unh, Mr. Hielscher," said Anonymous. "Is there anyone else at Northshore you cold talk to? Mr. Brady, Mr. Brady is unable to come to the phone right now."

"Okay," I said, and hung up. It was all I needed to know.

Here was I, under a name nobody had ever heard before, promising only the whiff of a job, and asking to talk to the honcho of the house. So am I told to screw off, or to write a letter, or to confirm my connection with the boss? No, I'm told that the boss isn't in, and I'm asked to talk to somebody else. Which meant that the secretary was either flustered, or coached, or both.

Ed Brady wasn't unavailable. He was gone.

I didn't know how gone, but I knew he was gone. With that kind of certainty you take to your dentist when you've got something about to be a bad toothache. (He usually, of course, tells you that you fancy the ache in the wrong tooth, but that nevertheless you do need a gold crown, price $400.)

"I think Brady's dead," I said to Marianne. "See if you can catch anything on the radio."

I have to give it to her—she was good. She flicked on the radio without a word, and waited.

The radio was tuned to an AM rock and roll station, and it was nearly five minutes till ten o'clock. Top-forty rock stations tend to broadcast their news at five minutes before the hour instead of on the hour. Don't ask me why, maybe it's a religious thing. Anyway, we didn't have long to wait. We listened to the last couple of minutes of some guy hollering about being born to run, and then to about a thousand comercials for furnace and mattress companies, and then the news began.

And then, when the news began, we heard, not really caring, about what was going on in Afghanistan, Oman, and another twelve or thirteen countries I could have done without, before we got to the local news. Fine. But the local news began with a discussion of the current snowstorm, and of how shitty life in Chicago is in the wintertime. And they call it "news."

At last we got down to the less important of the day's events. ". . . Police are investigating," hummed the lady reporter's androgynous voice, "the shooting, last night, of Edward Brady just outside his Kenilworth home. Brady, a former Chicago policeman and for the last few years head of his own private detective agency, was also one of the more prominent supporters of the mayor's last campaign and a fixture in Chicago political life. He is in the intensive care ward at Evanston Hospital, where physicians describe his condition as critical."

So much for Ed Brady. I hadn't liked him much in our brief acquaintance, and he had left me with some pretty large problems, personal and otherwise. But he had been alive, he had been a big, self-confident, arrogant, blustering Irish-style crook. And he had been shot, and maybe killed, in the city he was part of, and it was a damned shame. The most the radio could say about him was that he was a "prominent supporter" of the mayor's campaign. Well, terrific. Chicago, I've always found, loves its fixtures, its characters and its clowns. But it loves them when they're on the downslope. It's a city that likes losers the same way it thinks of itself as a loser all the time. It's the "Second City"—that's Chicago's own name for itself—and it's in love with being second best.

I turned off the radio, and turned to Marianne. "So much for my plots," I said. "That was Carp on the phone when I called Brady's house, and I thinkg he's going to be looking for both of us before long. Look. Things are going to start to happen soon, and I don't want you to be around when they do. So find Fred, Jr., okay? And we'll take him and you somewhere safe. I can think of a couple of places to call while you pack and get the kid."

But she just stood there, smiling at me. "Harry, Harry," she said. "You're not *thinking!*"

Why did everybody want to tell me that?

"Harry," she went on. And as she said it, she fluttered her

hands, like two gentle birds, to my face and then to my shoulders. "Darling. Just stop and think. Ed Brady is dead, or near dead, right? So everything he said last night is, well, *private*. I mean, only you and I know it, and Brady isn't about to tell anybody else for a long time, right? So," and now her hands were moving down my arms, "there's no need for you to tell Bridget O'Toole, or Carp, or anybody, about the plan, is there?"

Well, maybe there wasn't. At least, I told her I thought there wasn't.

"Of course there isn't!" she agreed. And now her hands were locked behind my back, massaging my lower back in ways the exercise shows on TV never even dreamed of.

"Of course there isn't! Now, Brady didn't give you a chance to look at the files on Fred's investigation, but I bet I can find some way to get them, or copies of them, for you. So, darling, why can't you and I *still* do what Brady wanted to do? You know? You go to them—the Wrights—and *you* get the money Brady was talking about. Couldn't you? I mean, if he's gone, we don't have to worry about trusting *him* anymore."

I swear to God, that's what she said: "If he's gone, we don't have to worry about trusting him anymore." I backed away.

Remember that movie, *The Shining,* where Jack Nicholson starts hugging that sexy nude in that spooky hotel? And all of a sudden, while he's hugging her, she turns into an obscene, leering old hag? It's how I felt. It wasn't just that the idea made me gag, it's that suddenly I didn't even want her to touch me.

"Jesus H. Christ, Marianne," I said. "You sound like Brady, only worse."

She was really shocked at my response, and that shocked *me* even more.

"But, Harry," she said. "It could *work*. And, just think, it could put you—it could make us—so *comfortable*."

"Comfortable," I said. "You think I'd be *comfortable* with somebody who could run a scam like that over two dead bodies? You feel comfortable letting Fred and Brady, and maybe me for all I know, go down the toilet so you can pick up some pin money? Is that what last night was for, to make me *comfortable* with this can of worms?"

"Harry, *no*," she said. "You're wrong. It's just that . . . that . . ."

"Don't tell me," I broke in savagely. "It's just that you love me and it isn't enough, right? Well, kid, for once you got it straight. It *isn't* enough. I'm going. If the police contact you, tell them any thing you want. I'm just going. I've *had* it, okay?"

And I left her, just like in a corny movie—but a different one than I'd started the day in—leaning against the goddamned corny icebox and about to start crying again.

Swell. She *had* meant well. It didn't make any difference. I was sick of people meaning well and doing rotten things to one another. And of everybody shoving the same stupid situation down my throat and telling me how dumb I was not to *see* what it all meant. And, I suppose, of myself. And since you can't kick yourself, as we all know, I did what any ordinary citizen would do, and kicked the person nearest me. What I want is to be left *alone*.

My car only died four times on me in the first three blocks, a sure sign of the coming of Spring. I had been awake less than three hours, and I felt like I'd gone through the whole day. First I'd admitted to myself something I hadn't thought in a hell of a long time—that I was in love. Then, by cup of coffee number five, I'd decided I wasn't. I wished there was somebody I could make pay for that: maybe whoever killed Fred and shot Brady, because I was sure it was the same person. But even if I—or somebody smarter than I—could "solve" the murder, would that really *mean* anything?

All the time Marianne and I had been cheating on my best friend, I'd never had a doubt that she and I were both, basically, nice people. It hadn't been a problem, you know? Now there was something—I couldn't quite get the word for it—something else. Maybe it was just that I'd begun to look at her like another human being, and that's always bad news.

I didn't know where I was going. I was sure Carp would want to talk to me again, and I was sure I wanted to talk to the Wrights again. Ed Brady's shooting, I realized, as I tried to keep traction under my tires, shot the hell out from under the anonymous mobster theory of Fred's death. So much for even thinking about selling it to the police or to the Wrights. Which left my tape, which nobody but me had yet heard, a phantom package of dope, that may or may not be behind the whole mess, and—I realized as I skidded to a stop at the corner of Sheridan and Hinman—not many options.

So I drove to the offices of O'Toole Agency, Incorporated.

• 17

OR AT least, I tried to. But something got in the way.

I hadn't gone four blocks when I realized I was being followed. By a large Buick Regal. That didn't skid on the ice. So I knew the driver must be somebody rich, because it's only rich people whose cars never skid on the ice, am I right?

Now, I don't like being tailed—nobody does—so I did what you should always do when you find yourself being tailed, and what hardly anybody ever does—outside my business, that is. I coasted to the side of the street, turned off my motor, jumped out of the car, and waited for the Regal to either catch me up or turn and run.

It caught me up. It pulled right beside me, and the door on the passenger side swung open. I could feel the warm air from the car heater billow out.

"Mr. Garnish," said a sexy, contralto voice. "May I talk to you for a moment?"

It was Yolanda Wright. She was wearing a giant looking fur parka, the kind of thing Eskimos would wear if they all had Lord and Taylor charge cards. It was thrown open to reveal a fuzzy pink pants suit that looked childish as hell and seductive as hell all at once—Marilyn Monroe's Doctor Denton's.

"Mrs. Wright," I wittily observed as I climbed into the car. "How did you find me?"

"Well," she said, dropping her voice another octave and expertly sailing into traffic, "let's say a little bird told me where you might be spending the night. And, frankly, I just assumed you'd be leaving Mrs. Healey's house about this time, so I waited down the block. Surveillance—no, stake-out, isn't that what you call it? And there you were! Don't you think I would be good at your business?"

As she said this she turned to me with the kind of smile they use to sell designer jeans on TV. And, tough, street-smart p.i. that I am, I realized in a flash that I'd just been abducted (again, goddammit!), that Yolanda Wright's convenient little bird was a tail I *hadn't* been sharp enough to notice, and that there was every chance the rich, pretty lady in the driver's seat was trying to run the moves on me. And I didn't care.

"And why did you want to see me, Mrs. Wright?" I said. "You could have left a message at the office, you know."

Her smile changed subtly. At least, I thought it changed subtly. Now it seemed to be saying, "Oh, you silly boy."

I hoped I wasn't wrong.

"Oh, Mr. Garnish," she said. "I really wanted to talk to you away from your well, your employer, and away from your ordinary business concerns. You see, I do trust you. And I hope you'll trust me, beyond the ordinary concerns of a client relationship. Oh, my goodness," she laughed, as she drove us, still expertly, wherever it was we were going. "Doesn't that sound impossibly formal and roundabout? What I mean, Mr. Garnish, is that I need your help. *Your* help, and not anyone else's."

Better and better, the beast inside me thought. "And what is it you'd like me to do, Mrs. Wright?" I asked.

"I'd like you to come with me, Mr. Garnish. I have a, well, a place in Evanston that I keep open for times when I feel like staying up here. Would you mind having a cup of coffee with me there, and listening to what I have to tell you?"

Would I mind? At that moment, the way I felt, I would have minded less having a hippo take a crap in my handkerchief. But to Yolanda I just said, "Fine."

We drove in silence to her "place in Evanston." It turned out to be an apartment building on South Boulevard, near the Evanston-Chicago border and, as I might have guessed, in the middle of a district where the monthly rent could have kept me in my own apartment for half a year.

Still in silence, we entered the place. It was a simple, clearly organized one-bedroom apartment. A living room, with a furry looking white sofa and two angular looking wood and cushion chairs. A kitchenette off the living room, where you knew you couldn't make anything more complicated than lasagna. And the bedroom.

Yolanda Wright led me into the living room and sat, the way a ballet dancer sits, on the sofa. She had shrugged off her furry parka at the door, so now she had on only her pink, sexy jammies. I chose one of the angular chairs across from the sofa; I still wasn't quite sure what was going on, and if what I hoped was going on was going on, I figured I'd find my way to the sofa soon enough.

As soon as we had settled down, she jumped up again and giggled like a kid. "Oh, damn!" she said. "The coffee! You just sit here; it won't take a minute. Or," turning at the kitchen door, "would you like something else? Something stronger?"

I couldn't figure out why, as soon as we'd entered the apartment, this cool, self-assured woman had turned into a nervous teenager. I mean, even if she was hitting on me—*why,* God knew—she must have been round the track enough times not to get starting-gate nerves. (I mean, I don't think I've ever been anybody's *first.*)

Well, it was her party. And a little taste might make things smoother for both of us. It wasn't yet noon, but the sun is always over the yardarm *somewhere* in the British Empire.

"Sure," I said. "Maybe a little Scotch, if you'll join me."

She giggled—no, really, giggled—again, said, "Coming right up," and reappeared a few seconds later with two glasses, ice, and a new bottle of Vat 69. She poured herself about enough to fill a petri dish and invited me to make my own. I poured myself enough to fill quite a few petri dishes. Her giggle turned into a warmer, throaty and comfortable laugh. Yes indeedy, we were on the right track.

"Honestly, you Irishmen," she smiled.

"Sorry to disappoint you, Mrs. Wright, but I'm a Czech," I smiled back. "They've discovered large booze deposits in Central Europe too, you know."

"Oh, no, please, it's Yolanda," she said, clinking glasses.

"Right. Yolanda," I said. "Now, Yolanda, nice as this is, what are we here for?"

Again, I thought she caught the hint I had tried to put in my voice (Garnish, you old fox!). And, again, she declined the gambit.

"Harry," she sighed. "I'll be as honest with you as I can. I hope you don't mind my saying this, but I really don't, well, I don't *like* your employer, Miss O'Toole. She's a bully, that woman. You know she bullied me into retaining your—her—services that day at the Hancock. And, though I'm sure she's not dishonest, there are certain things—certain things about this whole business that I would really rather not trust her with. I hope that doesn't offend you, does it?

I just mumbled something to the effect that it wouldn't drive me out the door.

"Oh *good*," she breathed. "Because, foolish as this may sound, I do trust you. Oh, I know we've only met once, and I know what you must think of me, because of all that nonsense with Knobby and, well and everything. But," and by God, she blushed. I'd always thought that past a seven-figure income you forgot how to blush. "But there is something about you, Harry, that makes me feel I—well, that makes me feel we could be friends, and that I could rely on you."

I set my eyes in their earnest, concerned, yes-you-can-tell-me-all look. An old girlfriend once told me I look like the "before" part of an Alka-Seltzer commercial when I do that, but it's the best I can come up with.

"Well, frankly," Yolanda went on, "I heard about Mr. Brady on the radio this morning. It's a terrible thing. He seemed such a nice man when I first approached him, and, of course, I'd met him before—at social functions."

I could believe it. Ed Brady wasn't your real Chicago purple, at least not the way the Wrights were. But he had clawed, donated, and politicked his way damned near the real purple level. So there was every chance that, once in a while, at the annual mayor's St. Patrick's Day Dinner at the Conrad Hilton or at some gathering to honor the visiting Prime Minister of Whateverland, he might have basked in real success, and been able to pass a dish of thousand island dressing to the President of Commonwealth Edison or Yolanda or Harmon Wright. The glittering prizes of life, right?

"Yes, Yolanda," I agreed, "it is a terrible thing. But is that why you wanted to talk to me?"

"Yes," she said. "I just want to know if you think that Mr. Brady's shooting has anything—anything at all—to do with Mr. Healey's death and with, well, you know, with *us*."

The way she said *us*, I couldn't be sure if she meant herself and Harmon Wright, herself and me, or just herself. But she had already hit a couple of false notes. In the first place, she had said that *she* approached Brady, which interested me just because I had assumed Harmon Wright himself would be the one to start an investigation of his own foundation. And, even more interesting and even falser, if a little bird had told her where I could be found that morning, it was a lead-pipe cinch that the same bird (who, I was sure, had red hair and a taste for bow ties) would have told her where I had been the night before. And that meant that she *knew* there was a connection. What was she asking for? Evidence of my stupidity or evidence that I was willing to play along, no matter what?

Every time I had made a decision lately it had turned out to be wrong. Well, that was nothing new in the Garnish family. My old man had emigrated to Chicago instead of San Francisco, after all, and had decided just off the boat, that the profession of mechanic was the wave of the future. In a city, mind you, crawling with out-of-work immigrants just dying to be mechanics. I decided to carry on the family tradition.

"Yolanda," I said, lighting a cigarette. "I'm not sure how much Brady's shooting has to do with your, uh, problems. But I talked to Brady last night"—she tried to look surprised—"and I can tell you that I'm sure there must be some sort of connection. Brady didn't say much about your case," I lied, "but he did indicate that there were complications in it that he didn't want to deal with himself, and that he hoped I—or somebody else—would take off his hands."

Her eyes were wide as saucers, and I was sure they were intentionally so. Nobody past the age of fifteen looks *that* amazed unless they want to. But that was okay; she was also breathing hard in her feigned amazement, and I was watching her breasts rise and fall, all draped in pink fuzz. It may have been a performance, but it was a damned good one.

We were quiet for a moment. Then she spoke. "Harry," she said, "I'm afraid of all this. I'm afraid that my husband *is* involved in some kind of drug traffic. I'm afraid that maybe he is using Ecology International as a channel for cocaine. I'm afraid—oh, Harry, I'm *afraid!*"

As she said this she started crying, and also held out her hands toward me. Like someone sinking in quicksand.

Well, enough is enough. I wasn't sure how much she knew, or how much she wanted to find out from me. But I know need when I see it, and I know loneliness when I see it. Without another word I took her hands and sat beside her on the sofa. She leaned her head on my chest, sobbed for a while, and then, all at once, before I was sure what was going on, her face was next to mine, and her tongue was exploring my ear, and I had found the midriff separation in her pantsuit, and we were walking and leaning against one another and stumbling toward the bedroom.

Sorry, but what came next is kind of a blur. If making love to Marianne was warm and cozy and comforting, making love with Yolanda was like trying to douse a fire with gasoline. I mean, I told you I know need when I see it. But her need frightened me; it was so damned *huge*.

Her body was everything I'd wanted it to be, and loving her was almost like dancing. I mean, she was always *there,* just where I hoped she would be. I felt like Fred Astaire below the waist. But her eyes—which she kept open when I kissed her—looked like she wanted not just to screw me, but to swallow me.

After I don't know how long we both lay back on the pillows, exhausted. Ever notice how that kind of time is, well *different* from any other time you know?

"Harry, you're *wonderful!*" she said, and I was too tired not to believe her.

"You're wonderful enough yourself," I said, stroking her cheek.

"Harry, you know, I hope we'll do this again soon." I hoped like hell she didn't mean in the next ten minutes, but didn't say anything. "I hope this won't hurt you, Harry," she went on, "but I do love my husband. My marriage is the most important thing in the world to me."

Oh Christ, I thought. What ever happened to the simple, uncomplicated lay? Why do people feel that, as soon as you go to bed with them, they have to open their souls just when what you're thinking about is getting your pants back on and having a nice cup of coffee?

"It's okay, kid," I said wearily. "I don't remember asking to move in with you."

"No, but really, Harry, I want you to understand. You're a— you're a wonderful man. I thought so the first time I saw you, and now. Oh," she moaned, and leaned over to kiss me. I sighed, wished I'd had Wheaties for breakfast, and went back to work.

I mean, sex starts at great and works its way up, right? But this lady had a taste for it that made me wonder if I hadn't been kidding myself about the Garnish gonads all these years.

Anyhow, after round two—and if there was a round three, I promised myself, I was going to claim an old war wound—we got back to Deathless Revelations. But this one *was* pretty deathless.

"Darling," Yolanda said (damn! I'd been promoted). "I just have to tell you this, all right? My husband is—oh, *hell!* I love him, Harry, but he's, he can't, we've never made love, Harry." And she turned her back to me and started sobbing.

I remembered Harmon Wright throwing things in his living room, getting murderous-looking crazy, and all of a sudden I felt sorry for the rich bastard. I remembered his passionate voice on the telephone. No wonder he went mad. To be married to, to love somebody like this, and not to be able to *love* this. I was glad it wasn't my problem.

"Look, kid," I said, stroking her still shaking back. "You don't have to tell me anything more, you don't have to explain a damned thing. It's okay, right? Just take it easy, and don't worry about things." I smiled. And she smiled back. It was a nice smile. So nice that I was beginning to wonder if maybe there couldn't be a round three, when the door to the bedroom opened and Harmon Wright walked in.

Remember those gag postcards on "What to do in the event of a nuclear attack"? They said, "Assume a seated position, lean forward, grasp your ankles, and kiss your ass goodbye." Well, it's not easy to sit up when you're stark naked and half-erect in a soft bed. But at least I sent my ass a quick telegram of condolence, with thanks for having stuck by me all those years.

The odd thing I noticed, even while I was trying to remember how to make a perfect act of contrition was that Yolanda didn't stiffen, gasp, scream, "Oh my God!" or try to dive into the bottom dresser drawer. She just lay—lie?—there. Grammer always deserts me when I'm facing extinction.

Wright, in a camel-hair overcoat that made him look, if possible, even more powerful and larger than usual, strolled to the rocking chair in the corner of the room, sat down, crossed his legs, and said, "Hello, Yolanda. I thought you might be here."

She smiled—really, she smiled—at him. "Hello, Harmon. Did you drive down yourself, or did Knobby drive you?"

He seemed to have discovered something very interesting about his thumbnail. "No," he said, "remember, today is Knobby's day off. I'm parked just behind your car, so I can drive you back home, if you like."

Nobody had looked at me or spoken to me yet, and I was beginning to think, suppose, Garnish, you just pull the covers over your head and be real, *real* quiet until they all go away. And then my luck ran out.

"Garnish," said Harmon Wright, "I know you're a heavy smoker. Would you like a cigarette?"

I didn't even have time to gurgle my acceptance (wondering if he was going to give me a blindfold along with it). He reached into my jacket—the right pocket, first time, the sonofabitch—brought out my pack, walked over to the bed, and shook one out toward me. As I took it—carefully not looking him in the face—he brought a gold lighter that appeared to be about the size of a Chunky candy bar, economy size, out of his overcoat.

Now, I've got a psychologist friend, Marge, whom I've helped collect fees from delinquent nuts a time or so. And Marge tells me that a very common "anxiety dream" (I love psychotalk) for people is that they're caught stark naked in public. "It's both a terror and a desire," she'll say, playing with her sherry glass. "To be finally, fully revealed for what you are, and at the same time to lose your artificial, public, clothed self."

I don't know for sure about all that. I've never taken Marge up on her offers to give me a free stab at analysis. But I can tell you this. Lying in bed next to a married woman, with nothing between your jewels and her wronged husband but panic and flimsy percale, is one of the goddamndest feelings life has to offer. And that you can take to the bank.

Yolanda spoke next. "Harry," she said, sitting up and pulling the sheet, thank God, around her. "You needn't worry. Harmon and I have an—an arrangement about things like this. I know it must be embarrassing for you"—Jesus, the woman was perceptive—"but, believe me, it's perfectly all right. No one will ever mention this again, and there will be no recriminations. Isn't that right, dear?"

"Of course," said her husband, still standing over me. And I couldn't help thinking what fun Bridget would have had talking about the idea of all this being "perfectly all right." "You see, Garnish," Harmon went on (why not first-name him, since I was almost family?), "I love my wife very much. And, as I'm sure she's told you—you tell them all, don't you, darling?—told you about my, aah, little problem, you understand that I can't really deny her her occasional, aah, forays."

The foray—me—just stared at the opposite wall, and said nothing.

"Of course," he went on, "I like to meet the men she, aah, fancies. Just to let them know, you know, that the, aah, convenience of the relationship is nothing more than that—and not to presume, you see, on that convenience."

Well, at least the lunacy of it all helped me find my voice. "Look, folks", I said. "I can take a joke as well as the next guy. But unless you've got another game you want to play with me, would you mind letting me get the hell out of here? See, I'm the only one not having any fun." And, as I finished my brave speech, I realized that Wright had again left me smoking without an ashtray. Ah, shit. I flicked a half-inch of ash onto their goddamned carpet.

Wright was smiling, not a nice smile. "No, Garnish, I'm afraid you don't get away with that easy self-righteousness. Yolanda?" and he handed her a robe out of the closet. She took it, slipped into it, and went off to the bathroom with her clothes in her hand. Not another word to me. I mean, I wasn't sure what the hell was going on, but I was sure that these two were practiced at it.

I thought Wright might maybe go red in the eyeballs when his wife left and jump on me, trying to rip my lungs out or something. I tensed accordingly, hoping I'd be able to brain him with the bedside lamp. But no such luck. He still had that calm tone of voice and his make-your-skin-crawl smile. I know, because I was still in nothing but my skin, dig, and it was still crawling.

"No, Garnish," he went on. "Do you think Yolanda's—*diversion*—with you makes the slightest difference in our marriage? Do you think I'm here to make you feel humiliated or silly? I just don't have to, you know; you matter that little."

I didn't know whether going from a foray to a diversion was moving up or down on the scale, but it didn't seem the time to ask. Wright was pacing up and down—on another of his highs, I thought, because I could see his eyes had taken on that gleam again.

"*That* little," he repeated. "What Yolanda and I have is something I don't think you could begin to understand, not even if I spent an hour explaining it to you. We have a full, a happy life together—a brilliant life, if you can even grasp the concept of that."

I wasn't insulted. I was just trying to figure out whether he was arguing with me, or with himself.

"And we have our work. The work I've hired you to protect, and a work that matters more than all the sweaty little affairs Yolanda may find herself involved in."

And since we'd come from talking about "forays" and "diversions" to talking about "affairs," I saw a chance to grab the whip handle. "So," I said, "this sweaty little affair is part of my job? I mean, this sweaty little affair helps lubricate the great work?"

It worked. He snapped his head toward me and the smile clicked off his face. And now I was looking at the face I'd seen the day before, the one contorted in pain just before he threw the expensive vase against the wall.

"Look," I went on. "You're bigger than I am and you're a hell of a lot richer than I am, and you've got me in the worst situation I can think of. Okay, Mr. Wright, if you want to beat the shit out of me, the points are all in your favor. But you've got to know that you've got one strange lady, there, Mr. Wright. But I'll keep working for you and, like the lady says, we'll just ignore this whole—what was it?—foray. Or better yet, leave me the hell out of it *all,* and I'll never see you again. I don't think we're likely to be in the same box at Soldier Field."

I could almost feel him relax. And it hit me, suddenly, that he wasn't worried at all about what I might tell anybody about all this. After all, who was I going to talk to—crumbs like myself? He was worried about what I might have said to Yolanda, or what she might have said to me, while we were in the sack together.

I mean, it was the kind of intuition you get sometimes when you're playing blackjack, and you're dealt thirteen, face up, and you decide to double anyhow. I knew that what was going on between Harmon Wright and his lovely wife had a lot more to do with what they did or didn't know about one another than it did with who'd been screwing the lady tonight or next week. This was something else altogether—something to do with the kind of absolute dependence they seemed to have on one another.

So, anyhow, Wright relaxed. "Oh, no, Garnish—Harry," he said. "You'll see me again, and you'll continue to work for me. Among other reasons, because I do want you to discover whatever you can about any—aah—irregularities at E.I. And, also, I have to say, because I want to impress upon you how unimportant this little affair really is to me and Yolanda. And, you know, Harry, I can *afford* to keep you on, just to impress you of that." But it wasn't like yesterday, when he'd told me "I know I can buy you," and I had felt slapped in the face. Today there was too much bravura in his tone. "And now," he said, "I expect you'd like to go. Is your car nearby?"

I told him not to worry about my car. He grunted and left the bedroom, closing the door after him. The bedroom door opened immediately—she must have been listening—and Yolanda, fully clothed, crossed to the living room entrance without looking at me. Me, I just lay there for a few minutes until I heard the front door to the apartment click shut. Then I got up, pulled on my clothes, and walked into the living room. It was empty, and the bottle of Vat 69 was still sitting on the coffee table. Poor little fella, I thought. Here we've all been having so much fun and we didn't even invite you to the party. Fuck them all, I decided, took a swig from the bottle, and went out to slip and slide on the ice all the way back to my car.

• 18

I WAS still feeling horny and confused—not a bad combination, by the way—when I walked into O'Toole Agency. But that all changed quick enough. There was Brenda, gazing at me strangely; there was Bridget, looking at me with an undefined warning in her eyes; and there was Patrolman Al Caceres, staring at me the way, I guess, a German Shepherd stares at a skirt steak.

"Well, hi, folks," I said. "Al, *Que tal?*"

Nobody smiled. "Harry," said large Al, "we've been waiting for you. Didn't spend the night at your place, did you? Anyhow, Carp wants to ask you some questions. I'm supposed to take you to him." Whenever Al doesn't respond to Spanish with either a joke or an obscenity, you know he's working.

On the other hand, Al was alone in the office. Now, cops always travel in pairs; it helps keep their life insurance premiums down. And the fact that Al, my old poker and drinking buddy, was here alone—he must have told his partner to wait in the car—meant, that, even though he was on business, and therefore couldn't afford to be friendly with me, he was still treating me like a friend. It was a delicate gesture, and I appreciated it.

I appreciated it so much that I decided to push it. "Swell, Al," I said. "But first you've got to tell me where Carp is, and why we've got to go see him."

Carceres sighed. He knew, and I knew, that he couldn't tell me why. He obviously didn't have a warrant for this pickup, and if he mentioned to me why Carp wanted to talk to me *without* a warrant, he could be liable to five or six different kinds of lawsuit. At least, if he didn't want to read me my rights before me told me why, and he didn't.

"Harry," he sighed. "Can't you just come along? You know

how the game's played, man. Why make a lot of trouble for everybody?"

I like Al Carceres. I like him a lot—about as much as I don't like Inspector Carp. But for the last five days people had been taking me places. And when they got me where they were taking me, it seems like they'd all gone out of their way to tell me how dumb I was for letting myself get taken there. Well, this time it was official. Thank God, this time it was legal, and that meant that I had something to say about whether or not, and where, I was going to be carted off to. Like Al Carceres or don't like Al Careres, I thought, but, dammit, this time you don't have to feel like a piece of meat.

I was just framing my answer to him when Bridget spared me the trouble.

"Office Careres," she said. "Of course, since you don't seem to have a warrant for the arrest of Mr. Garnish, we all assume that you're going to take him to an official place of interrogation and investigation. But just in case we have to get in touch with him during your interrogation, would you mind confirming that—before witnesses," and she glanced at Brenda, who didn't seem to know what the hell was going on, "and formally?"

Al stared at Bridget like he'd just met every cop's nightmare of an ACLU lawyer. "Well, Mrs.—Miss—O'Toole, ma'am," he stammered, "Skokie P.D. station is where he's going to wind up. But first I have to take him to Inspector Carp, and Inspector Carp isn't, right now, you know, at Skokie P.D."

I glanced at Bridget. It might be a way of getting out of the bust. But she wasn't having any, and she didn't return my glance. "Then, of course," she said. "Mr. Garnish will be happy to go along with you."

But enough was enough. "I sure the hell will *not* go along with you." I said to Al, "until you tell me what the hell this is all about, and why the hell Carp wants to see me, and where the hell we're going right now."

I get repetitious when I get excited.

Al's mustache got mean-looking. No, really, it did. I don't know how he manages it, but he can use his mustache as a means of assault, if not battery. "Harry, I don't want to make any trouble here . . ." he began.

"And of course there won't be any trouble, Officer Caceres," finished Bridget. *"Todos estamos amigos aqui, y usted lo sabe bien."*

I don't know if it was grammatical, but it sure the hell was effective. Al's mustache relaxed, and so did I. "Now," she went on. "Can't Harry and I confer for a few minutes before he goes off with you?"

I felt like it would've broken Al's face to smile at that particular moment. But he grimaced as gracefully as he could, and Bridget and I made our way to her office, with the Spanish-American walrus glaring after us.

As Bridget closed the door I noticed that old Phil was perking up. His five idiot faces were all erect, and were all a healthy green. I was about to mention something about that when I looked at Bridget's face. I shut up.

"All right, Harry," she said. "We've got ten minutes at most, and after that the only time we may talk is in a cell. With a lawyer present. So, dear, *what* is going on?"

I could have laughed. "Bridget, I was sort of hoping *you* would tell *me* what's going on." And I told her about my meeting with Brady, about his suggestion, and about my hearing about his shooting this morning. I left Marianne, mostly, out of it. Not out of chivalry. I'm just not a good storyteller, and I have to simplify all the time.

My boss listened. Then she stared for a while at her plants. Then she stared at me.

"Harry, Harry," she said. It wasn't that she was angry, it was that she was disappointed. "Why, *why* didn't you call me last night? Or even earlier this morning? I *told* you to call me."

I let it pass in sullen silence. If she could play nun ("Why didn't you finish your assignment, Harry?"), I remembered how to play fifth grade jagoff.

"Well, all right," she sighed. "You know I didn't want to carry this through to the end. But now I believe we have to put a stop to it, even if some people are going to be hurt. Here's what I want you to do. Go along with Mr. Caceres, and tell Inspector Carp, when you see him, that I would very much like to talk to him today. Tell him that I said I understand his peculiar problem. Tell him that I think the Trojan Horse can still be saved—make sure you tell him that. And then, when you're released—as I'm sure you will be soon, dear—please go to your apartment and get the tape Fred made for you. Bring it here, and we'll listen to it. Tell Inspector Carp, from me, that if he'll allow me to help, I think we can find what he wants within twenty-four hours, though—" and a frown passed across her face—"I'm afraid what we find won't be quite what he expects."

"Bridget," I said. "I know you and I have had our differences. I know you know I've resented your running the business, okay?"

I think it was the first time I had surprised her in two years. Dammit, she *hadn't* known!

"Well, anyhow," I hurried on. "Differences or no differences, you don't have to hang me out to dry, do you? I mean, you're asking me to give Carp—*Clarence Carp,* Bridget—a line like that? Wouldn't it be simpler just to fire me?"

She was genuinely shocked. In all that time we'd been together, she had never thought we might be enemies. And the thought of sending me on a suicide mission, apparently, was something she couldn't even imagine. What can you do with a woman like that?

"Harry, dear. You're tired and overwrought, so let's just make believe you never had to say those terrible things. Dear, I *can* bring this all to a head. And of course, Clarence Carp will believe me. Clarence, you know, was my best and sweetest student in the eighth grade at St. Athanasius. He'll remember me, and he'll know I don't make promises I can't keep."

I stared at Phil, who stared back. I hadn't known that about Carp. And, for Bridget's sake, I didn't feel like telling her what Carp had said about her at our last meeting. Or had he said it just to get me riled?

"Right," I said. "I'll tell your old eighth-grader about saving Trojan Horses, and he'll let me go, and then we'll just sail off and tidy things up like that," snapping my fingers. "Swell. But if you don't hear from me again within four days, call Calloran's, huh?"

She smiled. "Harry, it'll be all right, trust me. Any questions now, dear?"

"Well, just a minor one," I said, rising to leave. "Why was Fred killed?"

She laughed. "Oh, golly," she said, "you really don't know, do you?"

Bridget saying *golly,* by the way, is a sign of intense emotion. I'd only heard her lapse into that kind of language once or twice in our association, and you don't want to hear the equivalent in my vocabulary.

"Well, dear, I think it's best that you don't know—at least not yet. You may be asked to do—some things—where you'll be better off not knowing. Just trust me, Harry."

So who had a choice?

• 19

SURPRISINGLY enough, it went down just about the way Bridget said it would. Just about.

Al and his partner, who had waited in the car, drove me to Evanston Hospital where Brady was in intensive care with a lot of damage to his head and to one of his lungs.

Carp was waiting for me in the lounge outside Intensive Care. It was a strange meeting, because two or three other people were there, all looking haggard and scared. Obviously they weren't connected with our business, since they were scattered randomly around the tiny room, paying no attention to anything but their own worries. An older man and woman were huddled in one corner, whispering anxiously to one another. A pale girl sat in another corner, looking at nothing and smoking ferociously. Because it was such a public private place, Carp couldn't greet me as angrily as I was sure he would have liked to. He rose, nodded to Al, who left, and said to me, "Let's go get some coffee."

In the basement cafeteria he surprised me even more. He bought my coffee, and as we sat down he actually began by filling me in on what was happening. Ballistics had already confirmed that the same gun had shot both Ed Brady and Marianne. Ed Brady might make it, or he might not, and if he did make it, he might make it only as a vegetable. (Having only met him once, I still silently hoped that if that was the price, he wouldn't make it at all.) Mrs. Brady was at her home, under sedation and a doctor's care. Carp had known to look for me, as I expected, from Mr. Peter Getman, an employee of Northshore Agency, who had called him early this morning to tell him I was with Brady late last night. (So *that* was the real name of the mysterious Mr. Cacciatore.)

"We know, of course, that Marianne Healey was there too. But we don't need to talk to her, at least, not yet," he said. He was odd—quiet, subdued, depressed. I was beginning to get the uncomfortable feeling that he might be a human being.

"Garnish," he went on, "I don't especially like you, and I know you don't especially like me. Okay. Maybe I've gone out of my way to hassle you, and maybe you've gone out of your way to make my life hard. That doesn't matter right now. I want you to help me."

I didn't say anything. You can't, you know, with your jaw all the way open.

"The thing of it is, Garnish, my best friend is up there and may have half his head blown away, for all I know. And, goddammit, if he does, it's my fault! Do you have any idea what that feels like?"

I told him that I had some kind of idea what it felt like. "But," I said, "if you don't mind my asking, what do you mean it was your fault?"

Carp slammed the table with his open palm, and a little of the arrogant bastard I knew flashed back ino his eyes. Good, I can take change, but only as long as it isn't too fast. "Oh, hell, Garnish! Haven't you guessed yet? That whole line of crap Brady fed you last night was *our* line! You were supposed to feed me that horseshit about a mob killer, you dumb sonofabitch!"

A couple of nurses at the next table stared at us, then at one another. And then took their prune danishes to the *next* next table. Quietly.

"Unh, I know you're going to get mad when I ask this, Inspector. But why?"

"Why? *Why?* " He was getting so exasperated at my dumbness that he was getting over his guilt and mourning for his friend upstairs. One of the psychological works of mercy, I guess: pissing off the friends of the sick. "Because, dummy, we *want* to start that investigation of mob connections with the Wrights' charity, even if we do have to give the Wrights, or Harmon Wright, a front-row seat at it. Because it's *true*, dammit. There *is* a mob link. And the only way we can start a serious investigation is if we sell it to Wright as a way out of a sticky situation. And unless the Wrights are at least half willing to cooperate at the beginning, believe me, pal, there's no way we can even start. Now, would you like me to draw you a diagram to go along with that?"

"Oh," I said. He didn't need to draw a diagram. It was one of the oldest, and neatest, tricks in the book. Of course, there isn't any book, which is one reason the trick always works. If you want to catch a guy in a lie, tell him the *same* lie, but let him know you're sure somebody else is the liar. Nine times out of ten, he'll break his neck to cooperate with you, suggesting holes in the lie, contradictions—anything. Till, finally, you've got yourself a liar who has done everything but admit to the fact that he's a liar. And that last part is easy.

Could that be, I wondered, what Bridget had meant about the Trojan Horse? I mean, suppose you were trying to surprise the guys who *built* the Horse. Wouldn't you chuckle along with them while you were building it, and only at the last minute spring your *own* guys out of it?

"Oh," I said. "But, you know, I thought our meeting last Monday—was it only Monday?—was for you to find out if there was a connection between Fred and the Wrights."

Carp laughed. At least, I think it was a laugh. "For Christ's sake, Garnish. Man, we *knew* about the Wrights. Look," he said with a glance at the two nurses munching their danishes down the way. "What I'm going to tell you next is confidential. In fact, I don't even know why I'm telling you, except I know you're too smart, or too chickenshit, to pass it on."

Not knowing whether to bow or cluck, I sat quiet.

"What I wanted to find out when I interviewed you was whether you'd blow the whistle on Marianne Healey. And you didn't. That meant she was a hook we could use to pull you in, if we needed you. Okay?"

It wasn't okay. I was thinking about the way I'd left her, scared and sick and leaning against the refrigerator in her tacky kitchen. But Carp had the floor.

"Okay," he said. "We've suspected the mob connection with—what the hell do they call it?—Ecology International for months now. I mean, nobody goes into a cockamamie thing like that unless they've got something on the side, am I right? Anyhow, we planted a man in Wright's damn charity office a long time before they hired Northshore to run security checks. Not that I'm going to tell you his name."

"So, anyhow," Carp continued, "when they did hire North-shore for security checks, I thought and—and Ed thought—it was a stroke of luck. But it didn't turn out that way." Carp had lost energy again. He sagged visibly, and looked like he needed a friend. Unfortunately there *were* none—at least, not conscious and not within a five-mile radius, as far as I could guess.

"Inspector," I said. "What is it you'd like me to do?"

"I want you to go through with what Ed suggested. I want you to feed me information, that you'll get from Northshore, pointing to a gang killing of Healey. I'll buy it all, and then we can go to the Wrights and lobby for a public investigation, with them leading the hunt. And then, maybe, we'll find out what I wanted to find out in the first place."

"And the juice Brady—Ed—told me he wanted to get from the Wrights for all this?"

"Oh, come *on*, Garnish! You think we can get this past the Wrights *without* asking for juice? We want them to think that the investigation is a way *out*, man, a way out arranged by a greedy private cop with sloppy evidence, and something they can wiggle out of with a little cash. Use your head. Of *course* you go to them for juice. Now, will you do it?"

A couple of things struck me. The first, and I thought the less important, was this: we kept talking about "the Wrights," when actually it was just Harmon Wright, honcho businessman, who was supposed to be the possible target of this whole thing. But we kept saying "the Wrights." And Yolanda had admitted to me that she'd gone to Northshore.

The second thing that struck me was the absurdity of the whole thing. Here was an officially constituted officer of the law, in hot pursuit of a violation of the law. But his quarry was rich, and visible, and prominent. Rich enough, and visible enough, and prominent enough, that any hint of scandal or breath of evil was bound to be blown back on the man who originated it, even if it was true. So where did he turn? To a crummy private detective, and to a dumb inverse-blackmail plot, that's where he turned. I wondered how many other members of the ruling class had gotten away, maybe literally, with murder—just because there wasn't somebody as devious and as obsessed as Carp to worry them. And I found myself admiring Carp.

And, yes, there was something else. Here it was again, the story—the only sensible story—of why Fred had been killed. Yolanda Wright had hinted at it, Marianne half-believed it, Ed Brady had brought it up as a plausible lie or guess, and now Carp was telling me it was the truth behind the lie he and Brady had cooked up for me to swallow. And—aah, yes—something nobody else knew—the dead man himself had at least implied that it might be the reason he was a dead man. Hadn't he?

What bothered me wasn't so much the story itself, although there were some truck-sized holes in it. What bothered me was that so many people, for so many different reasons, seemed to want to believe it. It was the reverse of the bit about the blind men and the elephant. All my blind men were grabbing at different parts of the beast, sure enough. But they were all coming up with the same conclusion about its shape, and they *shouldn't* have.

"Will I do it?" I said back to Carp. "Yeah, I suppose I will if nothing better turns up. There's a friend I owe, too." Carp glanced at me and then, quickly, away.

"But there's a message I'm supposed to give you," I went on. "From my boss. I know it sounds crazy, but she said to tell you that if you'd call her today, she could help you clear things up within twenty-four hours. She said to tell you she understands your problem, and that she thinks she can still save the Trojan Horse. Now," I went on quickly, "don't holler at me about this. I know it sounds crazy, but that's what she told me to tell you."

His reaction surprised me even more than his acting like a human being had. "Twenty-four hours?" he said. "Okay, Garnish, we can wait that long before going to the other plan. Tell Sister—tell your boss I'll call her before one today. Now get out."

"You going to tail me?"

"What the hell for?"

"Well, thanks for the coffee."

I drove to my apartment and fished out Fred's tape. I wanted to hear it again, too. Then I drove to the office, where Bridget, Phil, and I listened to the whole thing, behind locked doors, at least three times. Then Bridget stared at nothing until I developed a cramp in my legs.

"Well," I said. "Any ideas?"

She shook herself. "Oh, dear—was I drifting? Excuse me, Harry. Yes, I think I know what we need to do next. We have quite a lot to do, you know."

"Aargh?"

"But I'm afraid we can't wait here for Clarence Carp's call. Brenda," she spoke into her intercom, "will you please tell Inspector Carp, when he calls, that I *had* to go out? And that I will call him back this evening?"

Brenda would.

"And now, Harry dear, I'll ask you for a ride." Funny, but she looked happy.

"Sure, Bridget. Where are we going?"

"Why, we're going to a *bar*." She said it with something like a schoolgirl's giggle at being safely naughty. "To be exact, we're going to the Bambi Bar."

That explained why she sounded so cheerful. It almost made me feel cheerful, too.

We were going to see the Judge.

• 20

I'LL tell you about the Bambi Bar first.

Remember what I said about the disappearance of the old-fashioned bar? Well, besides Ryan's on Wacker, a few do survive around Chicago. And the Bambi Bar is one of the best. It's right across McCormick Street, the border between Evanston and Skokie. It's a relic of the old days when Evanston (headquarters of the WCTU) was dry, so the whole town was ringed with bars and package stores, like Apaches circling the wagon train in a John Wayne western.

Those days are gone, but some of the old places still hang on, even though you can now get a drink in Evanston, too. The Bambi Bar, in fact, is both a package store and a bar. Why it's called the Bambi Bar nobody knows. There's a cute picture of Disney's Bambi hanging over the entrance, and some people guess that the Judge, its first and only owner, decided on the name because it was the cheapest sign he could get his hands on. Sometimes the Judge works like that.

Anyhow, it probably should have been named after Flower, the cute little skunk in the movie. Because the place always smells, like disinfectant at the beginning of the week and, at the end of the week, like beer and urine. In other words, all that grunginess that a place like Ryan's preserves so carefully and lovingly, the Bambi Bar doesn't have to worry about preserving. God made it to be grungy, the way he made sheep to be stupid and auto mechanics to be crooked. It's a birthright.

But Bambi's grunginess is legendary for miles around, and has been for years. (To the natives, by the way, it's always "Bambi's," as in, "Hey, man, what do you say we pop to Bambi's for some suds?") Half the polyester and black shoe junior executives, lawyers, and salesmen in the area got their high school eduation at Loyola in Wilmette, copped their first feel in the Northwestern stadium parking lot, and had their first legal drink, and a lot of others, in Bambi's. And of those three places, the one they keep coming back to is Bambi's. A couple of clowns who work on the Securities Market downtown even give an annual black tie dinner there. Seventy people in tuxes and formals take over the place one night, and sop up pitchers of Old Milwaukee and the Judge's homemade chili while they listen to Buddy Holly and Chuck Berry on the jukebox. Roots, you know? They take where they've gotten to back to where they came from. I don't see the fun—maybe because I never *got* there. But the Judge loves it.

Now I'll tell you about the Judge.

First, he's not really a judge, and never has been. His name is Gerald Solomon, and he's half Jewish and half Irish, which makes him, as he probably says once a day, a perfect living symbol of Skokie itself. Only, of course, he wouldn't say it that way. He would—and does—say, "Well, you know . . . I'm half Jewish and, aah . . . half . . . Irish and, aah, you know what that means, I'm . . . you know Skokie, so that makes me a . . . what do you call it? . . . symbol, I mean of . . . right?"

The Judge has never been known to finish a sentence. Some people insist that he's never even tried to start one. He talks in a voice like a stereo with a bad needle, and looks about like he sounds. As far as anybody can tell, he's never done anything except run the Bambi Bar. But "the Judge" is what everybody calls him. And not just because he wears black horn-rimmed glasses and has distinguished looking white hair flaring up all around his head. They call him the Judge because he's *smarter* than they are. Sitting there in his North Side bar with a nude calendar always on one wall and a Mickey Mouse clock on another—with two springs of palm stuck behind it every Palm Sunday—the Judge knows more about what's going on in Chicago than anybody else. Don't ask me how. He talks the way he does, in spurts and clusters of ideas, not because he's dumb, but because he just doesn't want to be bothered with having to arrange everything in a nice, clear order. He's the Judge, and he doesn't have to be bothered with that.

Some of the three-piece suits, in fact, come back to Bambi's as often as they do, not just to relocate their roots, but to get information from the Judge—business information, political information—that will let them keep going places besides Bambi's. And these are guys who are supposed to be in the know. People call him the Judge, in other words, because—weird as it sounds—they think he's a wise old man.

I've always called him the Judge, too.

Bridget and I sailed into Bambi's about noon. At that hour of the day, it's mainly populated by derelicts, carpenters, and painters out of work during the winter, and guys from nearby gas stations on a break. The place was far from empty when we got there. The fellow tending bar was a super-thin dude in a pastel shirt turned back at the cuffs, a mustache and beard, and tinted glasses. He looked like he would be more at home in southern California than northern Illinois. But, for what he was probably getting paid, I didn't think he could afford to dress any other way but like the wealthy, who like to dress like bartenders.

Bridget surprised me. She ordered a manhattan. I felt it was my place to uphold the family honor by ordering a martini. And as our drinks came, she asked the bartender, "Dear, would you ask Mr. Solomon if he could see an old friend for a few minutes? Tell him it's Miss O'Toole."

He sighed, shrugged, and trudged back toward the office. Life is hard for the working man, especially the working man who feels he's been screwed by his own past. He came back in three minutes to tell us that the Judge would grant us an audience. But he never got the chance. Because right behind him came His Honor himself, his right hand already extended as he left the office, a bundle of enthusiasm looking like a beachball packed into a blue pinstripe suit.

"*Bridget*!" he hollered as he strode toward us. "Well, my gosh, what a . . . you know, I was just . . . yeah, thinking about you, you know, oh, well, maybe four or five days ago! Well, darlin', come on in to my . . . oh, hey, hello there, isn't it Harry? My . . . my *office*!"

It's his way. And I've never seen him without the blue pinstripe suit, either. He must have a closet full of them at home. If he has a home.

We carried our drinks back to his office. His office is a cubby-hole in the back of the Bambi Bar, not a hell of a lot larger than the men's room. And it's rumored that a lot of the biggest and most complicated deals in Chicago have started there. Who knows?

Anyhow, he's made the cubbyhole into something like a library. Every wall is lined with volumes of Illinois Tax Law, state statutes, and legal journals. I think he subscribes to twenty or thirty of them. And on his desk, in the center of the room, was a Mr. Coffee machine, a pocket calculator, and a book spread-eagled in the middle, back up. I could read *Ulysses* on the spine, though the title was almost worn off from handling.

After the hugs and smiles were over—and that took a while—and we were all seated, the Judge poured himself a mug of coffee and leaned back in his swivel chair. "Now, darlin'," he said to Bridget, and suddenly the goofiness disappeared from his eyes, "what can I do for you?"

Bridget leaned forward. "Gerald, I need to ask you about Wright Enterprises. What do you know about their present situation?"

The Judge didn't change expression, he kept the same smile he'd worn since we met. But, while he kept his eyes on Bridget, his left hand reached out, closed *Ulysses*, and shoved it to one side of the desk.

"Why?" he said. Still smiling.

"Oh, Gerald," she sighed. "Surely you know what has been happening for the last week. First poor Fred Healey, and now poor Mr. Brady—you have heard about that, haven't you?"

The Judge nodded.

"Well, Gerald," Bridget went on. "I'm afraid I'm—we're—involved in it. Against my will, you know, but there we are. So I need to know, just to help clear things up, you know, if there have been any—unusual—developments in the Wright finances lately."

Still smiling like a damned lunatic, the Judge looked at her for a minute or so. He hadn't sent a word or a glance to me since we'd come into the office, but that was okay.

Suddenly, he laughed. "Well, Bridget darlin' . . . I mean, what can the harm . . . for an old friend like you . . . I mean, why not?" And he waddled over to a bookshelf and snatched out of it, almost without looking, what seemed to be a long, folded sheet of computer printout.

"Aah . . . you know I'm not supposed to have this. So you haven't *seen* me with this, all right?" He was unfolding the sheets on his desk as he said this. We both nodded, and I noted that, by God, he *could* make sentences when it was important for him to.

"Well, let's see, here," he rambled on. 'Aah . . . yeah, they're into . . . what you call, you know, *groceries*, the Wright people, you know? And . . . well, say what do you know? This is a, you know, a quarterly what they call report, and you know what it says?"

I would have reminded him that that's what we came to him to find out. But it was Bridget's party, so I just sat there saying nothing. Neither did she.

"What it *says*," the Judge continued, "is kind of . . . well, kind of *funny*. You know, young Harmon, when he started this whale thing, this save the whale thing, you know, he . . . well, he deferred, like we say, deferred, you know, a lot of his dividends from Wright, Inc. to the, the charity. Not a bad idea, hunh? I mean, if you got yourself tax-aah, tax problems, and . . . it's a kind of shelter, you know, hah?"

"Yes, Gerald, but *now*?" Bridget was maybe one of the few people who would interrupt the Judge's lifelong monologue.

"Oh, well, *now*! Well, now, you know, there's this funny thing . . . I mean, this is only a quarterly *report* you know, but if you asked me, I'd say . . . well, I'd say, you know, if you *asked* me, that there was something of a cash-flow problem with the, the *grocery* stores. I mean, what it is, you know, is that . . . well, you know, with prices climbing . . . I mean, you know what *lettuce* costs these days?"

"You mean," said Bridget, "the Wright grocery chain hasn't been doing well?"

"Well? Well, well no, I mean I can't really . . . I mean, it's not like they're goin' *broke*, darlin', or anything like . . . but you know who tried to buy them out a year ago?"

"No. Who?" That was me. I just thought I'd remind everybody I was still in the room.

The Judge, I guess, needed reminding. He looked at me like he'd noticed me for the first time.

"*Harry*!" he said. We couldn've just met after I'd spent five years in the Amazon. "Well, I can't really tell you, I guess . . . but, you know, they were . . . they are . . . *big*. And," he glanced back at his computer printout, just like it was a crystal ball. "And I don't think they'd make that offer today."

Another complete sentence.

"Well, thank you very much, Gerald," said Bridget. And finished her drink, and rose to leave.

That was it? I wondered. Why couldn't we have just called the old bastard, or for that matter, called any reputable stockbroker, if that was all we'd come to find out.

But maybe it wasn't all we'd come to find out. Before Bridget had gotten all the way out of her chair, the Judge stopped her.

"Now, *wait* . . . just . . . wait, darlin'," he said. "There's another little thing you ought to know if you . . . I mean, if you really plan to . . . well, you ought to know it, I guess. "Course, you understand, you never heard me say this, don't you—and you, too, aah, Harry?"

We never had.

"I mean, it's that Harmon Wright is, well . . . I don't know what you'd call it, except that he's . . . crazy, you know? I mean it's sort of like he's, you know, losing money all the time and just doesn't care. Just those damn whales and things . . . that's all, you know? . . . I mean, that's all he cares about. Lucky for him his wife, bless her, took over a lot of the bookkeeping before he started saving them damned whales. But, Bridget, what you ought to know is that . . . well, I wouldn't *push* him, or I mean, you know, crowd him a lot, hunh? He's *dangerous*, Bridget."

"Gerald," said Bridget, and now she rose all the way from her chair. "Gerald, I can't thank you enough. You know how much you always meant to Father, and all I can tell you is that you mean the same—and more—to me."

'Aah, honey," said the Judge, also rising from his chair. "Aah, you know what . . . well, you . . . oh, hell, darlin'." And he came around the desk and did something I'd never seen the Judge do to anybody, and something I'd never thought anybody would do to Bridget. He kissed her.

He not only kissed her, he ushered us out of his office like it was going to break his heart to see us leave. The flannel shirt juicers in the bar all turned their heads in surprise as he herded us to his special reserved seat at the bar and insisted we all three have one for old time's sake before we left. And when it turned out to be coffee all around, the juicers all went back to studying their beer foam and their fingernails.

There was the inevitable chat about old Martin O'Toole, and how he was doing now, and how much he was missed by all his old pals on the North Side. I kept out of it as much as I could. Actually, I didn't have to try very hard, because the Judge seemed interested in talking only to Bridget. I sipped my coffee and wondered what Marianne was doing now, and if Carp had decided to bully her yet.

Finally it was all over. There's a funny, not altogether healthy feeling you get leaving a bar in the early afternoon, even if you're not snockered, and even if you have been there on business. It's a feeling of being not altogether *right*.

Or am I starting to sound like the Judge, who, after all, owns the damned bar?

Anyway, as I tried to navigate my car across the ice floes that now spangled McCormick Street, I asked Bridget, "Did we find out anything we needed to find out, or was this just a social call?"

She, though, continued to stare straight ahead of her until we'd got safely back into Evanston space. And then she did speak. "Harry," she said. "I think you'd better get some sleep this afternoon."

I just kept my eyes on the road and kept on driving. "Unh, Bridget," I said. "Any particular reason, or do you just like to talk like the Judge?"

"Dear, you're going to need some sleep. I wish there were another way to do what we have to do, but I'm afraid you're going to have to stay up rather late tonight. Please drop me back at the office. There are some phone calls I have to make. And then, please go home, and try to sleep. Perhaps some whiskey would help. At any rate, come back to the office no later than—" she looked at her watch— "no later than six o'clock tonight. And do dress warm, dear."

Even I could sense the eagerness in her tone. "You really think it's that close to the end, then?" I said.

She sighed again. "Oh, dear, yes. It's very close to the end. I just hope it will *be* the end." And saying that, she stared out the window as if the passing, dreary expanse of Evanston might give her some kind of answer.

Me, I didn't even know the right question.

• 21

BUT I did go home, after dropping Bridget off, and I did get some sleep. Kind of her to think of it, after all. I hadn't gotten a lot—of sleep, that is—in the last couple of days.

Besides, I had lost track of what was happening. Nobody had even tried to kidnap me in the last five hours; my girlfriend, widow of the murder victim in the case (if there *was* a case) was, as far as I knew, no longer my girlfriend; and the Wise Old Man of the Mountain—or, at least, of the Bar—had told me that one of my employers in this whole business was going broke and crazy. And there was Yolanda.

There comes a time, I've always believed, when the best thing you can do is go to sleep. Actually, I feel that way quite a bit of the time. But since, this time, I had a second opinion, I knew I must be right. I went home, took a quick shower, opened a tin of sardines and washed it down with the last three fingers in my bottle of Scotch, snapped Paul Desmond into the cassette player, and crawled under the covers.

I didn't have to set the alarm, because I never sleep more than an hour or two in the afternoon. In fact, when Desmond finishing playing "Here's That Rainy Day" and the tape snickered to the end, I woke up and woke up all the way. It was three-thirty.

I poured yesterday's coffee into the pan on the hotplate, watched it boil, drank some down, and began to pull my clothes back on (I'd gone to sleep in my underwear, like any good soldier). In the middle of getting dressed, it struck me that I ought to call Marianne's house and make sure she was all right. I almost did it, too. But by the time I'd gotten my tie tied, I had decided to hell with it, and to hell with her. Life was getting complicated enough, and I was afraid, dangerous enough. I didn't need to stick my neck out one more time, especially for somebody who, I knew, if she wanted to try, could make me stick it out a lot farther than I wanted to. If you can't handle drink, stay away from bars, am I right?

So I muddled around the apartment for an hour or so, listened to some tapes, read a magazine, and made dinner—a can of ale and scrambled eggs with onions, Tabasco and Worcester Sauce. Don't knock it till you've tried it. By then it was time to report back to my boss.

Bridget was waiting for me on the outer office. She didn't look happy. "Harry," she said, as I came in to the reception room. "Did you get a good rest, dear?"

She always asks questions like that in a way that makes you know you'd better have had a good rest, because you're sure the hell going to need it later. I hate it.

"Oh, yeah, Bridget," I said. "I'm ready to wrestle a tiger, if that's what you've got in mind."

"Oh, *good*," she smiled at me. "Now here's what I want you to do . . ."

I didn't let her finish. "Bridget, no, wait, time out, just stop, will you? Before you tell me what to do, why don't you tell me what all those phone calls you made this afternoon were about, and what and I mean *what*, Bridget, is going down."

But I ought, by now, to know better than to try a frontal attack. She sighed, looked at the clock on the wall—it read six fifteen—and then glared impatiently at Brenda's unoccupied desk. She'd never suggest that my silly questions were wasting valuable time. Oh no, not Bridget.

"Harry," she said. "The phone calls I made this afternoon were to Inspector Carp, to Mr. Wright at his office, to Mrs. Wright at her home, and to, well, to someone else whose name I really can't give you right now, dear. And as for what is 'going down,' all I can tell you is that you'll be absolutely safe, I think, and that before the night is out I think we will have caught Fred's killer and put a stop to all this—this *silliness*." That last word she said in a way that made you think it was the worst phrase that could be applied to a human action.

I know when I'm beat. "Okay, Bridget," I sighed. "Since this is almost a real job, and since I almost think you know what we're doing, I'm almost willing to go along with you. What do you want me to do?"

She relaxed visibly. "*Thank* you, Harry," she said. "Now,

here's what I want you to do. At about eight or eight-thirty tonight, I want you to call this number"—she handed me a slip with a phone number on it—" and tell the person who answers that you are Harvey Wapner and that you have the package in question, and that you will be available to deliver it at midnight tonight, in the Skokie CTA parking lot. You will be standing, you'll say, under parking flag number 20. And tell the person who answers that you will only wait there for one hour. *Please* remember to say that, dear."

Flag 20 in the Skokie CTA lot, late at night? No way. I mean, criminals *don't* usually return to the scene of the crime, anyway. Forget what you read in your cheap magazines. But if they do, I for one by God don't want to be there *when* they do, especially if they're criminals who cut people apart with buzz saws. This was getting crazy. I was supposed to set myself up the way Fred had, in the same place Fred had, to trap Fred's killer. It was all so damned *dumb*, all so chancy, I couldn't even think of a reasonable way to tell her what a bad idea it all was.

"Okay, fine." I said. "*Do* you have the package of cocaine—or does Carp? And who's going to meet me tonight in the CTA lot? Come on, Bridget, even a wind-up toy like me needs winding up, you know."

She gave me what the Irish call, I think, a "straight look." She was obviously debating with herself, and I could tell by the expression on her face after a few seconds that my side of the debate had, for once, won.

"All right," she said. "You may as well know. The package of cocaine will never be found."

"Right," I said. "Why? Or why not?"

"Because," she smiled at me with that you-just-asked-exactly-the-dumb-damn-question-I-was-*hoping*-you'd-ask-smile. You ever see that one? "Because you can't find, Harry, what never existed in the first place."

"Right," I said. "Bridget, what the hell are we talking about?"

"What we're talking about," she sighed, "is blackmail. And blackmail of the ugliest sort. Not for money, that is, but for the sheer joy of giving pain."

"Fred?" I asked. And wished we were in Bridget's office instead of the reception room. I always look, I like to think, less stupid at moments like this when Phil is around for comparison.

"Fred?" she repeated. "*Fred?* Harry, Harry. *Think!*"

I swear to God it seems like that's what people have been telling me to do my whole life long. And the pisser is, every time they tell me that I really *try* to think.

"Right," I said. "Not Fred. Fred wouldn't get into anything like that, is that our line? So who? I mean, who's blackmailing who—whom—and what happened to the pack of coke that Fred mentioned on the tape that, you tell me now, was never there?"

That smile came on again. She was going to get to explain why $a^2 + b^2 = c^2$ for any right-angle triangle. Better yet, she was going to get to explain it to Joey Lobotomy, class dunce and inveterate nose-picker.

"Oh, Harry," she beamed. That beam—I hate it—always means I've just stepped in the dogshit on the lawn and she's going to pretend not to notice. "Think back to poor Fred's tape. Did he say anything about cocaine? He did not. He called the package an 'insurance policy,' and that's all he called it. It was Mrs. Wright who invented, and foisted upon us, the fiction that the package contained cocaine. Remember Fred, Harry. He was—well, rather a puritan, wouldn't you say?"

I would.

"Yes. Well, then. A puritan, and a man almost frightened by the very things it was the nature of his business to deal with. Of *course* we can't imagine Fred as a blackmailer. Perhaps it's unfair," she continued, staring at a spot somewhere a foot above and to the left of me, "perhaps it's unfair, but I've always thought if he hadn't married, hadn't gone out into the big world, had stayed celibate . . . Perhaps he had a vocation to the priesthood. Lord knows, it can be a refuge for the terrified as much as it can be a beachhead for heroes."

I was fascinated; I'd never heard her talk like this before. And, even if I suspected some of it might be nonsense, there was something in the conviction of her voice that made me want to hear more. But she stayed silent after that.

"Unh, okay, Bridget," I finally said. "So there was no coke from the beginning, and so there was no package from Fred. I mean, look. I'm about to get my ass waxed, and I don't like the idea of getting it waxed for a bunch of things that don't even exist. What is there—what do you think *is*—going down around here?"

Bridget didn't exactly smile this time. She just sighed herself a little deeper into her chair. And that's not easy to do when the chair is a yellow plastic number from K-Mart.

"Oh, yes, Harry, there was cocaine, I'm afraid. There's been cocaine all along, just as Inspector Carp believes—though not, perhaps, as centrally involved in things as Inspector Carp believes."

Aargh?

"It's just that cocaine, you know, isn't really what Fred had to bargain with."

"Right," I said. *"Bargain,* you said. Then he *was* blackmailing somebody, Fred was."

"Harry—really! Sometimes I think you're being deliberately obtuse just to tease me. There are an infinite number of reasons to keep an object, or a piece of information, besides blackmail. Can't you—really, now—think of any?"

The one that immediately came to mind was to use the object, or piece of information, to beat Bridget O'Toole about the head and shoulders with it. But I could think of another one, too.

"Okay, sure," I said. "To protect yourself. To save your ass, keep your bacon unsmoked, keep you head out of the sh—out of the water. So if that's the reason, what could Fred have had in the damn package?"

"Good, Harry! Very good! He could have secreted, for his own protection, information *about* a blackmail plot. About who *was* blackmailing Mr. Wright and about how the blackmail was being—what's the word?"

"Run," I said.

"Yes, *run.* Remember, dear. Fred was, well, I hate to say this, he was such a timid soul, and such a romantic besides all that . . . Well, suppose that he had somehow discovered who was blackmailing Mr. Wright. Wouldn't he, don't you think, foolishly try to secrete or conceal information about what he knew to be a crime, and couldn't quite bring himself to expose as such?"

"Bridget," I said, "I'm sorry, but I don't think we even know for sure that Harmon Wright *is* being blackmailed. And, believe me, I've had a few more chances than you to talk to the bastard." I shivered a little, remembering myself bare-assed under the covers staring up at our hero in his overcoat.

"Harry, Harry," she shook her head, "Didn't you listen to what the Judge told us? Mr. Wright may not be a nice man, but he's a *troubled* man. The Judge understood that—could read that—from the records of Wright Groceries and E.I. And, of course, we can guess why he's troubled, what he's trying to do about it, and why now he's even more deeply troubled than he was before."

Well, it was fine with me. I know damned few people who can understand what the Judge is saying, let alone what he's implying. But if Bridget could, why fight her about it? I even knew a guy once who swore he could predict your future by reading your license plate number.

"Swell," I said. "So H. Wright is getting jacked for the coke connection. So Fred tumbles to it and stashes the evidence on the jack-artist—what, a cancelled check? A letter? Whatever. So the artist finds out, and slices Fred for his trouble. Or hires somebody to do it, if he's smart. And then tries to ice Marianne, and Brady, and probably me, tonight, for the same reason. Am I doing okay so far?"

She just nodded, serious and encouraging. I was cruising for a gold star in my notebook.

"So," I went on, "excuse me if this sounds really dumb, Bridget. But if you're right about all that, then I can only think of one candidate for the blackmailer."

She was nodding harder now, as violently as one of those mechanical drinking birds you see in liquor store windows, before I'd even finished the sentence.

"Yes! yes, Harry! Mrs. Wright!"

And suddenly I was angry. Don't ask me why. I had no stock in Yolanda and she sure as hell had no claim on me. In fact, at that moment, I realized that all along she'd been coming on to me like a vamp in a forties film—Barbara Stanwyck in Guccis, for Chrissake—and that, like the classic horse's ass my old man always told me I was, I'd been buying it—retail.

But I wasn't angry at her. I was angry *for* her, the way I'd been angry for Bridget with Carp. As I say, don't ask me why. Maybe I've got this thing about ladies I sleep with. Or maybe it's just a thing about ladies I figure have got enough trouble already.

"Oh, hell, Bridget, that just doesn't make sense!" I was on my feet, pacing the office and fumbling for a cigarette. "You really think Yolanda would—*could* be that screwed up? Why the hell should she blackmail her husband when she's got all the bread she could ever need? I mean, God damn it, she *loves* the big dumb bastard."

"Loves," Bridget repeated. And sat very still, not looking at me or anything else, as far as I could tell.

"Loves," she said again, in a tone of voice that made me stop pacing and stare at her, the cigarette halfway to my mouth. "Harry, dear, I wonder if you know what that verb means, or if you know—*can* know—what strange things people are capable of doing because of it. How old *are* you, Harry?"

"Forty-two," I said automatically. I was surprised enough by the question that I couldn't even think of a smart-ass answer.

"Forty-two," she nodded to herself. "And you still think that loving can't be also a matter of hurting—or causing pain for the joy of causing pain? At forty-two?"

The way she asked it, I didn't really want to answer her. And the way she asked it, I realized why I'd gotten so angry. It wasn't that I was angry for Yolanda's sake, and certainly not that I was angry because Bridget's idea seemed to be irrational. No. I was angry—and, dammit, I kept *on* being angry—because if Bridget was right about Yolanda blackmailing her own husband, it meant that in a crazy way she really *did* care about him.

I sat back down.

"Okay," I said. "We'll pass on the question of emotional maturity"—Christ, I was starting to talk like her—" and we'll agree that Mrs. Wright is the crazy buzz saw killer. We'll even agree that after making Fred Healey into shiskebab"—Bridget, as you might expect, winced—"She pegged Marianne and Ed Brady just for the hell of it. Or just to save her tail from a charge of— what would it be, Bridget? First-degree murder for the purpose of obstructing justice? Or blackmail compounded by bodily injury? If I was a cop, I couldn't even make out the rap sheet on what you're suggesting."

But she wasn't having any. She just stared at me, didn't say a word.

"Right," I said. "So who am I calling to meet me tonight—to return to my first question—and why?"

She could not have looked at me more strangely if I'd just sprouted avocado shoots from my earlobes. "Why, dear," she said, "you're calling to alert the killer."

Oh.

But the killer, you think, is Yolanda, right?"

"Dear, I didn't *say* that." Shyly, almost with embarrassment.

"Oh. Sorry. And, excuse me if this sounds stupid, why am I being Harvey Wapner instead of Harry Garnish, when I make this call?"

"Oh, Harry," she chuckled. No, really—she *chuckled*. "Because I don't want you to *compromise* yourself, dear. And also—if I'm right about things—I don't want you to alert the killer to the fact that we've, we've *got his number!*"

She seemed so damned proud of herself for having found that phrase that I didn't even want to remind her that the killer was a *she,* not a *he.* "And besides," she went on, though I hadn't asked her, "Harvey Wapner was the name of a boy I used to date. *Goodness,* that was long ago!" she stared somewhere into the wall over my left shoulder. "And it just seemed, well, you know, *fun* to use his name for an, an operation like this, don't you think?"

I was speechless.

Well, not quite. "Right," I said. "And when I meet the killer—Jeezus, Bridge, *when I meet the killer?* What the hell am I supposed to *do?*"

Sigh, sink into plastic chair, look like a cantaloupe on vacation in Florida, and generally be an unhelpful pain in the—no, in *my*—ass.

"Oh, dear Harry." I had never, in all my months of working for her, felt less reassured by her Mother Superior tone of voice. "Oh, Harry," she repeated, "don't you think that we'll have provided for your safety? Inspector Carp and I are going to make sure that nothing untoward"—*untoward?*—"happens to you. Just relax, dear. Everything will be all right."

Why didn't I trust that? Okay, okay, I know. Because Sister Mary Joseph told me everything would be all right, back in the seventh grade, back in Holy Cross Grammer School, back on the near North Side of Chicago, the afternoon the tornado came and ripped the roof off the school, the traffic lights off the street, and the confidence out of Sister Mary Joseph. "Harry, dear—go home," Bridget said.

"Go home. Right," I said.

• 22

I DIDN'T feel like going home. For one thing, I had to make my damned phone call. And, though nobody had mentioned it, if the people we were going up against were as powerful as everybody said, then there was no reason they couldn't have my home phone tapped—which, of course, could screw up the whole operation.

At the word, "operation," I caught myself. Terrific, Garnish, I thought. "Operation" you're thinking, just like a junior G-man. What you are is a decoy, a balsa wood duck, with about as many brains and less balls.

Besides, home was too far to drive.

So I drove to the Bambi Bar, the package side, not the bar side. I go there a lot, but not as much for the booze as I do to chat with Manfred, the night man. Manfred Wilson is his full name. He's 6'1", black, balding, and if Sean Connery was as black and as smart and as agile, you'd say Manfred looked like Sean Connery. He's as much of a friend as I had, after Fred and Ben Gross. And I felt like saying hello to a friend.

We chatted for a while about some old bebop musicians. As usual, Manfred not only knew all their records, but had met half of the names we dropped. The place was practically empty, except for a forlorn looking girl, who couldn't have been more than sixteen, staring at the cheap wine rack and casting anxious glances at Manfred and me. Underage, scared, and desperate for a taste. Both of us pretended not to notice.

It was while I was saying something I thought was really smart about the great trumpeter, Fats Navarro, that the girl grabbed a bottle of Chianti and ran out of the door. Manfred shouted after her and charged to the edge of the counter, but then stopped and strolled back. grinning out of one side of his mouth. "Ahh, *shee-*

it," he said, "that girl's going to feel worse tomorrow than I could *ever* make her feel tonight. So—you were saying, Harry?"

Manfred's a philosopher. A good one.

But I'd already cost my pal some inventory, and it was past eight-thirty, past time for my phone call. So mumbling something dumb, I walked to the pay phone by the door and dialled the number Bridget had given me.

I wasn't really surprised to be talking to a machine. A voice I'd never heard before said, "You don't need to be told who this is. If you have dialled the correct number, leave your message after you hear the tone." There was a beep, I left my message, hung up, and walked back to the counter where Manfred stood, staring at me strangely.

"You got trouble, Harry?" he asked.

I've never been a good liar. "Manfred, I said, "I've got trouble. More than you really want to hear about, okay?"

"O.K.," he said. "Your business is your business, man. Just don't, you know, forget you've got *friends,* huh?"

No. I didn't hug him. The counter was too high. I thanked him for his time, told him I'd be by again the next night (not believing it for a second) and, as an afterthought, bought a pint of Vodka to shove in my overcoat pocket. It was a cold night—ten degrees was tomorrow's predicted high—and I didn't know how long I'd be in the CTA lot.

There's a twenty-four hour hamburger stand across from the lot. I parked my car under flag twenty at 10:00, walked and slid across the street, drank four cups of coffee that tasted like parboiled carbon, and by 11:30 was back in my car, waiting for a killer to come after, God help us, Harvey Wapner. I couldn't see any police support or surveillance, and on Dempster, on a winter midnight, you ought to be able to see anybody. To a professional, of course, that was reassuring, since it meant the cops were working at top form, totally concealed and ready to move at the slightest hint.

I had never felt less like a professional.

11:45. There was no point sitting inside the car, since the heater hadn't worked right all winter. So I stood outside, freezing my ass off, dancing like a punk rocker, up-down, up-down, and trying to ignore the pint of vodka in my pocket. It was too early to get sloppy.

12:00. I wondered where Marianne was and what she was doing there. I wondered if I still had feet. I wondered, if I start my car, would the heater warm up before the tank ran dry?

12:15. Mouth gone. I tried to say "Bob blows balloons" three times, and all that came out was "Bluh bluh bluhbluh" and a lot of steam. I unscrewed the vodka top, took a killer swig, and spent the next few minutes watching the streetlights dance. They were very good, I thought.

By 12:45 I figured the evening was a bust, and I wasn't all that sorry. I'd done the right thing, stood up for justice—and in fifteen more minutes I could get away without it costing me anything. If anybody was coming after me they'd have come by now. It was like that feeling you used to have on roller coasters or in horror movies, when you were a kid: you were sure the worst was over, and now you could relax and coast to the exit and tell your friends, "Aah, it wasn't all that bad."

Of course, that's when things always got worst, right?

At 1:00 or thereabouts I was certain nobody was coming. As a reward for heroism, I finished the vodka and turned to open the car door, hoping the car would start. And noticed a pair of headlights turning into the lot. It was a VW Beetle.

The hell with it, I thought . . . It's 1:03, and the doctor is through for the day. All murderers please apply tomorrow for another appointment. My hand was shaking, and not from the cold, as I fumbled for the ignition key and the Beetle sailed closer.

But then again, I thought, suppose Bridget and Carp really were right about this whole thing? Suppose a good friend of mine had been killed because of, for Christ's sake, a cash-flow problem? That's what the whole thing came down to. And did I have that many friends?

The VW had pulled beside me. It was an old one. Even in the crummy CTA lights I could see rust spots all along it. It sat there, purring. I couldn't see who was inside, and I knew that whoever was inside knew that I couldn't see.

It was funny. I mean, really, funny hah-hah. I probably could have jumped in the car, driven the hell out of there and that would have been that. I mean, car chases like in *Bullitt* and *The French Connection* don't happen in Chicago in the winter.

And I swear I don't know why I did what I did. I don't think I want anybody to tell me why I did what I did. Maybe I just wanted to find out if the Skokie P.D. and Clarence Carp were as damned good as they thought they were.

Anyhow, what I did was step up to the waiting car. And as I did, the door on the passenger side swung open. I could feel the warm air from the heater billow out as I leaned down.

Sorry, folks, but I don't remember a lot of what happened after that. I leaned in (thinking Harry, you *dummy*, as I did) and saw a bundled-up figure behind the wheel. The figure was pointing something at me and I hoped to God it wasn't a gun. It didn't look like a gun. It looked like Mrs. Yolanda Wright was going to clean her windshield.

Then two funny things happened.

The first funny thing was that Yolanda Wright spoke to me in a man's voice. "Hello, Garnish," she said in a baritone.

The second funny thing happened while I was trying to adjust to the first funny thing. It took less time to happen than it takes to tell it now. Harmon Wright—that's who it was, folks—hit the top of his windshield spray and, don't you know, it wasn't window cleaner at all. I was still trying to think of something to say when I noticed my legs weren't working right. Then my mouth was dry, I began seeing colors instead of things, and then all of a sudden I was with Marianne, on a tour boat of the Caribbean, sipping a mai tai, heading for a day in St. Thomas, and everything was lovely, lovely, lovely.

• 23

THE real kicker was that when I opened my eyes, it wasn't Marianne I saw but Bridget O'Toole. Her cantaloupe face was wrinkled with worry, and I couldn't see anything else. But I could smell hospital.

"Harry, dear. Oh, goodness, it's so good to see you conscious again," she said. "Listen, the doctors say you inhaled some sort of nerve gas. You'll be quite ill for a day or so but—thank God—there should be no permanent effects."

Well, I thought, "conscious" might be putting things a little strong for the way I was feeling. I've given all night mouth-to-mouth recsuscitation to a quart of gin—lost the sonofabitch, too—and felt better the next morning than I felt just then. But I decided not to quibble, especially since I wasn't sure I could talk. So I glared.

And it worked. By golly, it worked. Bridget got flustered. "Oh, Harry," she stammered, "you mustn't think that you failed in what we—I—sent you to do. You were *wonderful*, Harry! Even to that nervous pacing beside your car and that—that vodka bottle. How did you think of that, Harry? It was such a convincing touch. It gave you just the right air of uncertainty and vulnerability."

Indeed, it was a perfect touch, I thought. But I didn't think Bridget needed to know how I had thought of being really uncertain and vulnerable.

By now I'd decided that, if I tried real hard, I could probably utter articulate sounds. And I did.

"So it was Harmon Wright all along?" I croaked.

"It was everybody all along," said a harsher voice than Bridget's. "The only trick was finding out where the hell everybody came into the goddam thing. Unh—excuse me, Sister—I mean, Miss O'Toole. But you did O.K., Garnish. I'll give you that much."

"Huh?" As my eyes remembered how to focus, I could see Clarence Carp standing behind Bridget. It was he who had spoken. I tried to unfocus my eyes.

"Right," said Carp. So much for going back to sleep. Carp was in the mood to give a lecture, and nobody—except, of course, Bridget—is harder to stop when they're in that mood than Carp.

"Right," he repeated, rubbing his hands together and beginning to pace up and down my hospital room. "This was one of those cases, Garnish, where the real problem was sorting out the shit, not finding out where it was buried. Know what I mean?"

I knew what he meant—most murders, really, turn out to be like that—and I also knew that if I'd been closer to conscious I would have told him he was a hopeless garbage mouth.

"So," he went on. "We knew that Wright was running his little coke importing deal, and we knew he *was* using E.I. or whatever the hell he calls it to cover the smell. And we knew—thanks to your boss here, and none to you, Garnish—that somebody was jacking Wright around about it."

"I had to tell Inspector Carp, Harry," Bridget put in. "Don't you see, without that bit of information, none of this would make sense?"

I felt too damned sick to forgive her. Hell, I felt too sick even to be mad at her.

"Now the question was, who was blackmailing Wright, and why," Carp went on. "And the answer was, his wife, because she's fuckin' crazy. We got her in custody now, and I can tell you, that's one weird lady. Admits she was blackmailing her husband, and insists she was doing it because she loved him. Wanted him, she says, to give up the damn save-the-whales stuff, and just get back into the grocery business, where their goddam *money* was. Doing it all for his own good, you know? And get this—Wright knew she was jacking him off."

"Huh?" I said. It was about all I could manage.

"Yeah," Carp went on. "See, your pal Healey found out that Mrs. W. was the blackmailer. But what he didn't find out was that good old Harmon W. already *knew* that. So Harmon iced your friend to protect his goddam—sorry, Ms. O'Toole—his goddam blackmailer."

Sick as I was, I couldn't let that one past. "Wait," I croaked "Wright did all this to protect Yolanda?"

"All of it, dear," Bridget said. "Every bit of it done out of a perverse love. Well, maybe not even perverse. I suppose that depends on your idea of what the limits are between loving and hurting. But, you see, the famous package that poor Fred had secreted, and that he thought would be his—his insurance policy, as he called it—was exactly the opposite. It insured his death. Because he didn't realize that Harmon Wright knew his wife was blackmailing him, and would do anything to keep her from being exposed as a blackmailer."

"And Marianne?" I said. "And Brady?"

"Both shot by Wright," Carp said. "Or, at least, by people Wright hired to burn them. Maybe they were mechanics, maybe they were amateurs on Wright's payroll. We really don't give a damn, Garnish, about that—we'll never find them, anyhow, and anyhow we got the guy who paid them. You dig?"

I didn't dig. There was some kind of warning, or some kind of evasion, in Carp's voice that I wasn't used to. Like I say, the Chicago cops aren't any better or any worse than any other big city force, on the whole. But they don't normally let loose ends like two unexplained shootings just *drift*. And Carp seemed to be just letting it drift. And Brady was, for Christ's sake, one of his few friends in the world.

"Yeah," I tried to say, and it came out halfway between a whisper and a whine. My head felt like an overinflated balloon the moment before it bursts. "Yeah. So you got Wright, and you got Yolanda, and you don't give a flying fuck about who else may have been burning folks lately, on account of you already got the biggest fish in the lake, damn near pan-fried out of the water. What is it, Carp? You think I'm so goddam sick I've gone stupid?"

Count the words if you want. I haven't, but I know that none I ever said cost me more. I was gasping when I finished, and I let my head sink back on the pillow and closed my eyes. I just wanted everybody to go away.

They didn't, of course. "Harry. Dear." And I felt a soft, pudgy pair of hands take one of mine. Guess who.

"Harry," Bridget went on, "please don't excite yourself. Inspector Carp has been very concerned—haven't you, Clarence?—about your health, and he's simply telling you that some, ah, details, of this investigation are not likely to be as easily resolved as some others. You know, Harry, it really isn't a perfect world. And sometimes we do have to make adjustments to that fact."

What the *hell*, I thought. Now Bridget was sounding evasive, too. And then everything was cleared up for me by another voice, a voice belonging to somebody I hadn't seen in the room before.

"Yeah, boopsie," the voice said. "Just thank your stars you got out of this with your ass in one piece. You know, that Wright was about to fire up the buzz saw again before I got to him."

"Bridget," I said. "What is Knobby doing here?"

"Dear," she said, "Knobby was the—the other person I called. He saved your life, you know." And she blushed. And I knew why. "Excuse me" she said, "I must go call Marianne. She wanted to hear the moment you were conscious. Oh, Harry, I'm so happy you're all right." And she leaned over, kissed me on the forehead, and plumped out of the room.

Leaving me alone with Carp and Knobby. Maybe, I told myself, I'd be generous since Knobby had saved my life. Maybe when I got out of the hospital I wouldn't hire a couple of guys I knew to kick the shit out of him.

Or maybe I would.

"What is it?" I asked. "State's evidence or just a deal with the Grand Jury prosecutor?"

"Huh?" said Knobby.

"Huh?" said Carp.

"Aah, bullshit," said I. "You know what the hell I'm talking about. Knobby, you shot Marianne and you shot Brady and you did it because Wright told you to, and I'll bet my ass you picked up the key to Healey's package at the bar before I set foot in the place. And you couldn't give the package to Yolanda or to Harmon Wright because you were working for both of them at the same time, and you didn't know who to trust—or maybe who to blackmail yourself, you little shit." My head was *killing* me as I finished, and I felt like I had to throw up. Some heroic speech, am I right? I lay there gasping like a landed salmon.

Knobby was the first to speak. "Hey, boopsie," he said. "You know, I don't know what the hell you're talking. Your boss called me, asked me to do her a favor, and gave me some good reasons to do it. Saved *your* ass, too, you know?"

And Carp said, "Garnish, you're sick. You're tired, and you're sick, and you never did have too many goddam brains to begin with. So why don't you just forget what you just said, and go the hell to sleep, and when you wake up, try to make believe you ain't more of an asshole than anybody else on the street. This investigation is over, you got that?"

"I got that," I said. "And Knobby, thanks for saving my bacon. And Carp, thanks for the advice. And now both of you get the hell out of my room."

And crashed asleep.

• 24

I WOKE up Friday morning, about six. I was still in Evanston Hospital, but I was damned if I was going to stay there.

Evanston Hospital isn't a hard place to sneak out of if you have no sense of personal hygiene. I pulled on last night's socks, yesterday's underwear, shirt, etc., and before Nurse could come by to check my whatever, I was on my way to the bus stop.

Which I took to O'Toole Agency. Somehow, I didn't feel like going to my apartment. And besides, downstairs from O'Toole Agency is Ben Gross Dry Cleaners.

Ben was reading as I walked in, something called *Entropy*. And the samovar was steaming. And I was feeling like maybe I wasn't so damned smart to have left the hospital, because my legs didn't seem to be doing what I wanted them to do.

"Harry," said Ben, and rushed around the counter to take my arm and lead me back to the card table that served as his desk. "You look like shit, my friend. You want something to eat? Some tea, maybe?"

I told him that what I wanted was to sit and talk for a few minutes. But Ben is Ben. So I got tea anyway.

"Nu," he said. "I heard about your trouble. They let you out of the hospital already?" Then he looked at me closely, and immediately said "So they didn't let you out. That was silly, Harry. So why are you here?"

"Ben, I said, "I don't know, except I want to ask you something. I've been mixed up with five or six people who've been as ugly, lately, as any people I've known. And the reason they all give for their ugliness is that they're in love You ever been in love, Ben?"

He sighed. "Have I been in love? Yes, Harry, with a few people and with a lot of ideas. And with one woman, very special.

I never told you about my wife, did I? Ah, you should have seen her. But—but things happened." And things happened then. As he said that, his eyes got moist. And he held out his right arm to me. The arm with the numbers on it.

"Oh, Christ, Ben," I said. "I'm sorry, man. Look, let me just get out of here—"

"No, no," said Dr. Benjamin Gross, late of the University of Ingolstadt. "I'm all right. It comes and goes, you know? But look Harry, loving somebody don't mean you're all the time happy. And it don't mean you do beautiful things all the time, just because you're all the time seeing hearts and flowers. Have I been in love? *Yes,* dammit. And it hurts now worse than anything I know. And I wouldn't have traded it for anything. You understand?"

Probably I didn't. Ben, I think, always understands more than I do. But that's okay. He's older than I, and I've still got time. Don't I?

Anyway, as I climbed the steps of O'Toole Agency, I thought about Yolanda Wright. She'd done what she did for love. And I had done some stupid things for love, too, to another woman. And I'd done them because she loved me, which is to say acted human, which is to say acted crooked, for me.

I had loved Fred. I could say it, now he was dead. And I loved Marianne. And Yolanda and Harmon Wright had loved one another. And out of all of that, what had come? One life gone, two about to be wrecked, and two others hanging in pain.

As I climbed the steps to O'Toole offices, I decided that it was all silly. Why bother trying to keep up a feeling that was probably crazy anyhow, and probably just the result of some random collisions of atoms any shrink could explain away? It led to murder, didn't it? And to doubt, guilt, betrayal, and a state of mind like a constant toothache? I was better off without it.

And there, in the office, was the Friday doughnut party. Bridget, beaming, Brenda, wolfing, and—since business was so good we seemed able to take on more help—Knobby, smiling his ass off.

I grabbed a bear claw and some coffee and excused myself, walking to my office. I wanted to call Marianne. I hoped she'd be at home.